MARIE-HÉLÈNE LEBEAULT

AUTHOR OF THE EVERS SERIES

BLOOD MAGICK

BLOOD MAGICK BOOK 2

BEACHES AND TRAILS
PUBLISHING

About the Author

Positive, uplifting books and stories.

Marie-Helene Lebeault lives in Quebec, Canada and is the mother of two young adults. A retired teacher, she now spends her days writing, translating academic manuals, and lending her voice to corporate training videos. She enjoys reading, hiking, and going to the beach. She is also an avid rollercoaster fiend and is on a mission to visit all the Six Flags amusement parks with her daughter. Every year, she travels for three weeks on a solo adventure to a new part of the world.

Follow on Social Media, she'd love to hear from you!

Website Email Newsletter

ALSO BY THE AUTHOR

The Evers Series

The Ancestors' Key

The Academy

The Time Walker

The World Jumper

The Complete Evers Series Box Set

The Blood Magick Trilogy

The Blood Mage

Blood Magick

Blood Legacy

Standalones

Clarity Castle

Anthologies

What Happens Next?: Readers Decide Which Story Becomes A Book

Novellas

Stranded with a Shifter: A YA Holiday Romance

Picture Books

Fairy Grandmother: Millie Goes to Antarctica

Fairy Grandmother: Millie Goes to the North Pole

Fairy Grandmother: Millie Goes to China

(Available in English, French, Spanish, German, and Italian)

CHAPTER

ONE

THE BLOOD on Tom's hands sizzled and spat like butter in a hot pan. Tom felt the heat collect in his chest as his pounding heart pushed fire through his veins. Power pulsed to the tempo of his beating heart. It was frightening and invigorating. The air around him crackled with energy as though lightning was stored in his chest ready to explode. His senses sharpened.

He could hear the chanting outside. As he looked, the wards shimmered and wavered. The Master stood outside of the gate, his black robes billowing in the winds. His outstretched hands looked as though they were reaching for the gates. Three neat rows of ten disciples behind him mimicked their Master with outstretched arms. Their eyes were closed in concentration and their combined power was beginning to weaken the wards. The wards were failing, Tom feared.

Tom supposed he should have been terrified. After all, Harding Academy had sent Witches to the Callahan residence every day for a week to set and strengthen them, layer by layer. The dark magic The Master and his minions wove was stronger than the wards. They would gain entrance to the house soon enough.

Tom braced himself for a fight. He felt his body tremble. If it was from fear or from the power coursing through him, he couldn't tell.

Perhaps it didn't matter. He planted his feet firmly and willed himself to calm down. The Warlocks attacking the wards weren't teenagers. They were fully grown men and women, very likely trained by The Master himself. Each and every one of them was probably stronger than Tom was, in more ways than just brute force. They knew more spells, probably ones he had never heard of. Dark spells no one was supposed to use.

He spun in a slow circle, trying to work out how to set things to protect himself. The second-floor landing gave him a clear view of the front door and entranceway. *What if they came through the bedrooms?* They may have been minions of a dark Sorcerer, but surely, they could still scale the walks and enter through one of the bedroom. Tom raced down the hallway, opening every door he could find. They weren't going to sneak up on him!

He might have thwarted their plans once before, but it was doubtful they were here to kill him. At least, Tom had hoped his powers were still too important to them. It would give him precious moments to fight back as they tried to take him alive. Every part of Tom's body trembled. The Professor should have been back by now with reinforcements. *Was the Master so powerful that he could stop Doors?* The thought sent another wave of chills through Tom's body.

He pulled himself back. He couldn't afford to be distracted, couldn't allow himself to panic. Tom looked around the landing for possible weapons or tools. Mirrors, paintings, knick-knacks all received his assessing gaze. He thought that he should have a plan, but none came to mind. He filed away the inventory for future reference. What else did he have?

Professor Montague had taught him a few defensive moves. The truth was, he hadn't learned nearly enough. Certainly not enough to prepare him for such a confrontation. He mentally ran through the block and shield maneuvers. Taking a deep breath, he prayed that he could hold down the fort until help arrived.

Tom had spent weeks learning to control his emotions, while tamping down his anger so he could focus his Magick. He could hear the Headmaster advising caution in the back of his mind, but this was different. Tom allowed his blood to boil now. His family was at stake.

When his mother was shoved through the Door to safety, he willfully forgot all of that and allowed his blood to boil. Professor Thunderbolt had looked back at Tom and gave him a nod of encouragement. As soon as he stepped through to the relative safety of The Academy, the Door had vanished.

The weight of the Key Tom wore was reassuring. He was a Traveler, after all. Escaping this place would be as easy as summoning a Door from nothing and vanishing in an instant. But this was his home. His family's home. His father's home. Tom would not and could not give it up so easily. Not after everything his family had been put through. He was ready to fight but he needed a plan.

The chanting at the gate grew louder. Under the cadence, Tom heard the gate begin to creak open. He took another deep breath and tried to center himself. Looking out the window, he saw the house wards still held and took some comfort in that. Still, they were not as powerful as the ones at the gate, the ones The Master had already obliterated.

He had a wild thought. If his Blood Magick could be integrated into the wards, would that strengthen them enough to buy him time? Professor Thunderbolt had promised to return with reinforcements, Tom only needed to delay long enough for him to return. Tom was alone. He would never ask a friend to put themselves in harm's way. The sheer number of robed Warlocks, not the least of which was The Master, made it far too dangerous. Tom felt that he had a chance to put an end to this before anyone else got hurt.

The part of his mind that was not concentrating on the wards raced with questions. How could The Master even *see* the house? The wards were supposed to hide the house from those not invited. That was what the Witches had promised, were they wrong? Was The Master just that strong, or was there someone at Harding Academy working against them? If so, who? He began going through the roster of people he had met at the new school and, to his horror, realized that he had lost focus and the wards were failing again.

He poured more energy into the wards and felt the house shake as the wards fought to stay put against dark forces. The house moved like it rode an earthquake, doors and windows rattling. Somewhere, glass shattered. The light from Tom's energy poured into the ley lines from both sides, and it grew painfully bright. Tom's eyes burned and itched, and a pinpoint of blinding pain exploded in the back of his head, growing to a searing pounding. He was too afraid to look away, lest he lose focus again but just then, the light flared, forcing him to automatically shield his eyes.

THE CHANTING STOPPED. For a silent moment, Tom stood in utter darkness. His eyes were so used to the blinding light that no longer existed; they took their time adjusting to the relative gloom. He strained to hear any sounds while waiting to see again. But outside, the Warlocks had gone as silent as a tomb. The hair stood on the back of Tom's neck and goosebumps chased themselves up and down his arms. As his eyes found their focus again, the only sounds were the tick-tick-tick of the grandfather clock. He tried to look in every direction at once. There were no sounds. No chanting. Nothing. Tom realized that the eerie silence was more unnerving than the chanting.

He took a cautious step to the edge of the landing and looked down; his eyes locked on the door. He reached out tenuously with his mind and instantly recoiled. He could *feel* The Master on the other side of the door. They seemed to be waiting for him to make a move, but Tom was biding his time until the Professor's return. Besides, he'd learned from playing chess that sometimes it was better to wait and allow your opponent to make his move and reveal his plan. His stomach churned and the acid caused by fear ate away at him. When the clock chimed, he yelped and nearly jumped off the landing.

As if that were a signal, the front door flexed, and a large BOOM ran through the house. The door shook on its hinges as the Warlocks slammed some sort of battering ram against it. Tom willed himself to wait, embracing his anger and rage. Another BOOM tore through the house, but this time, he could hear the wood splinter. Tom knew that the door could not withstand another such assault.

With one more BOOM, this one had a sour note, interrupting the dark symphony of chanting with a shatter. The front door burst inward, sending splinters into the floor.

Warlocks ran into the house like roaches fleeing the light, their robes flapping around them as they paused to assess the room. He knew they were looking for him. He fought the instinct to run and hide. Fear began to overwhelm the anger until he had to force himself to stay where he was. He concentrated his energy and reached out with his mind. He gathered the shredded pieces of the door and flung them at the robed intruders. Some fell, while still others tangled up in each other, struggling desperately to stay upright.

"He's up there!" One of them pointed to where Tom was standing. Tom suddenly realized that his attack had only revealed his position. Maybe he shouldn't have struck first. *Am I going to hell for that?* For a moment, he wondered if the Blood Magick was making him meaner. *Am I evil?* His powers always worked better when he was angry, after all...

He shook off that thought, time enough for pondering that, if he survived the day. He willed himself to remain calm. They had broken down the door and entered his home, but they had not yet tried to harm him.

The others clustered around the one who had spotted him, and all their faces turned up to look at where Tom stood. He could only see shadows under the hoods of their robes. For a long and surreal moment, no one moved, they only stared at each other. Tom wondered what they were waiting for, but the answer came soon enough when a gravelly voice called out, "Get him!" The words sounded more tired than angry, but the single phrase broke the tableau. The Warlocks threw themselves at the steps like the running of the bulls.

Tom reached out with his mind again to throw a console table down the stairwell. The front line of Warlocks fell like a row of bowling pins and Tom couldn't help but laugh. The ones in the rear, however, continued unhindered and were definitely not amused. Tom heaved an enormous wardrobe in their path, but one of the Warlocks flicked his fingers and it spiraled over the railing, shattering on the floor below and doing no harm to those on the stairs.

Tom wished he could turn the steps into a ramp, hopefully a slippery one, and watch them all fall over each other. Short of that, he began throwing everything he'd noticed before: paintings, knickknacks, vases. Nothing he threw stopped them, but his actions certainly slowed them down. Tom sent out a plea for Professor Thunderbolt to show, and quickly.

"Just grab him and be done with it!" that same gravelly voice called out, exasperated.

Tom couldn't see the source of the voice, but every Warlock he'd set down jumped up again and renewed their advance. Clearly, throwing things at them wasn't a winning strategy.

The memory of the blast that had saved him in the dungeon returned to him. Could he recreate that now? If he pushed out the shield and threw it at them, what would happen? The better question was, could he do it again if it wasn't *exactly* a life-or-death situation?

An orange ball of energy made its way toward his head and Tom was almost relieved to see it. Well, they *were* shooting at him, so to speak. He whipped his arm up, the shield materializing to protect him. It must have been a test to see if he could use defensive magic because suddenly, it was raining fire and light. The Warlocks had just brought the attack to a new level. The gloves were off now.

The energy balls filled the air and Tom had to shift to ensure they didn't make it past his shield. *They're using my own tactics against me. I'm busy fighting off these blasts while other Warlocks are getting past my defenses.* Thirty against one. It hardly seemed fair. Surely there were rules for this kind of thing. He felt the anger return, warming him. He embraced it. Blood pooled in his hands and his face burned. His skin was ablaze with rage and his stomach churned molten fury.

While his left arm kept the shield in place to block the spells and fireballs, he reached his right arm back as though gathering air and pushed pure energy at the attackers. They flew back and down the stairs, landing in a pile at the bottom of the staircase.

This only seemed to anger them more. They renewed their assault, bombarding him with a new wave of fireballs and spells. Tom deflected them easily enough, but the cost was beginning to show. Keeping up the shield hadn't required much energy, but his counterattack had wiped him out. He couldn't keep this up for much longer. The breath he dragged into his burning lungs scorched his throat and he began to lose hope.

Meanwhile, The Master was losing patience.

"Enough of this nonsense!" The Master's voice took on a new note of fury. Even the sheer volume of his exclamation did not disguise the rock-grinding sound of his voice. "This is taking far too long!"

Tom felt a chill run down his spine when he realized how close this voice was. The shout had come from inside the house.

The Master had arrived.

CHAPTER
TWO

"LEAVE US."

The silence following the assault was absolute. Again, only the idiotic *tick-tick-tick* of the grandfather clock dared to interrupt the slow shuffling of feet as the Warlocks filed out. Tom's ears were filled with the sound of blood, precious blood, coursing through his veins and the heat of the breath he dragged through his parched throat.

Tom edged closer to the railing to catch a glimpse of his nemesis. There was no one there.

Only when the last of the Warlocks shuffled through the open doorway, did The Master cross the threshold. He strode in casually, as though he had simply stepped out for a moment and was back for a visit. His hood covered his face, making it impossible to see much of him, but a wicked and vicious sneer showed just under the edge of the cloth.

The Master glanced around the room and shook his head. He tsked at the damage and shrugged. "Never send boys to do a man's job." He looked at the rubble at his feet and made a dismissive wave of one hand. The shattered pieces of the front door quivered and rose. They levitated for a moment, flew past him, and rearranged themselves into a door. The Master gestured toward the door. It closed with a solid thud, a reassuring sound that it was complete again. "Now we have some privacy."

Privacy? Tom swallowed hard. *Stall. Stall for time until help comes.*

The Master took in the rest of the rubble, the shattered wardrobe, the smashed knick-knacks. "I do apologize for the mess."

Tom found himself unable to speak, he only nodded mutely.

"Jameson was right." The Master lifted his head to stare at Tom from under the hood. "You *are* quite powerful, aren't you? I must admit, I am impressed. Your time at Harding Academy has been well invested." He waved his right hand, a small gesture, barely a flicker, and the pieces of the wardrobe reassembled themselves. In moments, the wardrobe rose majestic and gleaming and settled itself in the place it had sat for many years. If anything, it looked newer, better than it had been.

"You'll be an excellent pupil." Another wave and one of the vases suddenly righted itself on a corner table, the shards blending until the fracture lines were gone. One by one, the debris of the fight floated this way and that, returning quietly to their proper places. Perhaps this was the most disconcerting thing of all, that The Master would care about Tom's home.

"Now, enough of these games. I'm going to ask you to come along." There was an edge to The Master's words. Though his stance was relaxed, almost bored, Tom could hear the steely command under the seemingly benign words.

"I told Jameson I wouldn't join your cult." The defiant words came out in a croak as Tom forced them past his lips, which seemed too dry. The Master said nothing, but his hand flicked to the balcony near Tom, and something rattled behind him.

The decorative suit of armor, one of the things The Master had reassembled, had moved. Slowly, as if waking from a deep sleep or raising from the dead, the piece shifted. Its movements were jerky and hesitant. The limbs flexed oddly, as if trying to snap old bones back into place. The cold that suddenly ran through him caused Tom to shudder and he found himself unable to swallow.

Do something. You must do something.

Somehow, Tom raised his hand and formed the shield again, pushing it against the metal Gollum, as he had done against the Warlocks. Instead of being propelled back, the empty armor merely paused for a moment and then pressed through Tom's defenses as if they weren't even there. He risked a glance at The Master, but the man was still on the first floor, that ever-present self-satisfied grin glowing from under the hood.

The animated armor kept coming. Slow yet steadfast, it closed the distance. Tom's shield was useless against it. The monster kept coming.

Echoing laughter rose from the floor below.

"I can *smell* your fear," The Master hissed. His words sounded from every corner of the house, without direction, without source. It filled the spaces and reverberated from the clanging, clinking sounds of the armor as it drew closer.

The armor swung its sword in a deadly arc heading for Tom's neck. It was surprisingly fast and very lethal. *He is trying to kill me!* In that instant, whatever confidence Tom had gained from telling himself that they only wanted to take him, had now vanished. Tom ducked, dancing out of the blade's path. The creature lunged, with another blade aiming for Tom's belly. He slid out of the way, and the tip of the blade took a slice of his shirt. He pushed energy toward the enchanted armor, hoping to knock it over, but all it did was absorb the shock. The armor didn't so much as tilt under the blast.

"I'm not afraid." Tom spat the words defiantly. His shout was meant to bolster his own courage more so than to defy The Master. Not that it worked in either capacity.

"Your eyes call you a liar." The Master's voice laughed at him from everywhere at once. Again, the armor swung the blade, this time a sweeping arc that would have opened Tom from neck to belly had Tom not dropped to one knee. He felt his panic stirring, there was no way to defeat this monstrosity. No magic touched it. Everything he threw at the monster was absorbed. He couldn't play dodgeball with a sword indefinably. A magical construct would never get tired, and it certainly wasn't going to stop.

Tom was about to spring to his feet to dodge the next assault when he saw an opportunity he'd been missing. Tom grabbed the edge of the rug and yanked it with all his might. It was enough for the creature to lose balance and topple to the ground in a heap of metal.

That was too close. It was more than enough time to leave. He'd been arrogant enough to believe he could go toe-to-toe with The Master. Cursing himself for a fool, he grabbed for his Key, but it wasn't there. In a flash, the chain was ripped from his neck. That's when Tom knew true fear. There was nothing, absolutely nothing more terrifying for a Traveler than to be without their Key. Tom clutched at his throat as though he'd been strangled.

The Master laughed in triumph, dangling Tom's Key like a bully playing keep away.

"Where is your boasting now?" The Master taunted him. "Or are you truly afraid?" He shouted with laughter, the cowl shaking with mirth. "Come down and fetch it." He spun the Key in lazy circles. "You have great untapped potential, my son. Join me, allow me to teach you what *true* power is."

It was as though the house itself was talking to him, the sound coming from the walls and ceiling and floors until Tom was deafened by it and couldn't think beyond the single phrase, which seemed to hang in the air between them.

True power? Power enough to protect those he loved? Power enough to bring The Master to his knees? Tom turned the words over in his mind. Could he learn long enough to overpower him and take his place? His family would be safe forever....for a moment, he was tempted. He could almost taste how good it would feel to have that kind of power at his fingertips. To never have to worry that he couldn't protect someone he loved ever again.

Tom brought himself back. That was not the answer, and he knew it. The temptation was real enough. Feeling this vulnerable and help-less were enough to drive him to accept the offer, but he dug in his heels and raised his head boldly.

"I will *never* join you!" He screamed these words at the hooded figure, even as he reached for the Key, Tom demanded that it return to him. The Key tore itself from The Master's hand and flew back to him.

Did The Master show some pain when the Key was wrenched from him? "AND I AM NOT YOUR SON!" Tom's voice rode the wave of renewed power that coursed through him as the Key nestled safely in his fist where it belonged.

He felt strong. Powerful. The Magick coursed through him, glowing under the surface of his skin. It was addictive. Mesmerizing. Tom was almost drunk with the power. It was also *wrong*. It was dangerous. A mistake. Evil. Evil felt so good. It occurred to him that The Master wanted this, wanted to let Tom feel the extent of his power, wanted him to feel rage and anger and hate, because with each breath of negative emotion, the power grew in him, demanding to be set free.

He wants me drunk on power. He wants me to get addicted and demand more and more until I agree to join him just to get it. Tom tried to calm the anger in him, to take deep breaths and still his heart. *I won't give him the satisfaction.*

He faced The Master, his power coming under control. He hadn't heard the armor rising from the floor, hadn't seen it reassemble and walk toward him. He saw it now, only briefly, as the sword swung through the air. He managed to fall back, but not in time. Instead of taking his arm off, the tip of the sword cut into his upper arm and lay the muscle open. Blood poured down his arm as Tom screamed in pain.

This time, the shield worked. He felt the difference, like going from a feather to a sledgehammer. The armor slammed through the upper railing and shattered into a cacophonous pile of dented scrap at The Master's feet. The Master didn't so much as move and none of the pieces struck him. He laughed again.

Tom grabbed his arm with the other hand, blood on his fingers, and willed the healing to begin. He felt a hand grab his good arm, an iron grip that nearly broke the bone. One of the Warlocks was behind him. Either he had hidden and was biding his time, or he had re-entered through a bedroom. Tom fell into the training from his Martial Arts class and spun, intent on pushing down on the man's arm while twisting his trapped hand. They grappled and twisted apart, but at a cost. The man's fingers scrabbled, trying to regain their grip, closing instead on the ring around his finger. The signet ring twisted and came free, popping over the knuckle under protest, scraping some of Tom's skin with it. Tom lunged after it, but the ring flew through the air and landed somewhere behind them.

The distraction proved deadly. He whirled on his attacker, furious at the loss of the ring, enraged that he was being attacked in his own home. The outrage boiled his blood and as Tom raised his hand against the other man, he felt the wrongness of it. But something was happening that he could not stop, not even if he wanted to. He and his opponent froze, watching in horror as Tom's blood slid down his arm, over his hand, and congealed into a long, pointy spear. In a panic, Tom tried to jerk his arm back, but the spear only kept getting longer.

The blood spear glided, unhindered, into the Warlock's chest. The man's eyes grew wide with fear, pain, and shock. The Warlock made to grab for Tom's hand but missed and staggered back against the wall. Unable to stay upright, he slid to the floor, leaving a smear of blood on the wall behind him. The blood spear had run him through.

"MASTER!" The man screamed, clutching at his heart to staunch the crimson flow.

Tom fell to his knees. The sight of what happened, of what *he* had done, overtook him and he threw up on the mahogany floor. As he retched, he didn't notice the blood spear liquify and pool around his hand. The tingling in his fingertips prompted him to open his eyes and look down. As though being sucked through a straw, the blood climbed over his hand and traveled lazily back up his arm, seeping quietly into the closing wound like a plane returning to its hanger.

As the wound was replaced with pristine skin, Tom realized he could heal the Warlock. He fought to his feet. "Hold on," he croaked, "I'm coming." Before he could take a single step, The Master's foul voice stopped him cold.

"Kill him." The Master hissed from the floor below. "Kill him. It's the humane thing to do."

Tom forced himself to take another step toward the injured man. "You're insane! I can heal him!" It only then occurred to him that all this might be a trap. It was a setup to capture him. His survival instinct told him to summon a Door and run. Could he leave a dying man to his fate without trying to help? No. He couldn't.

"How does it feel to hold the power over life and death in your hands?"

Tom whipped around. He'd been so accustomed to the booming voice that came from everywhere, that the whisper caught him by surprise. It sounded as though The Master was standing closely behind him and breathing into his ear.

His own wounds had closed, and his hands were clean. No. Not clean. Tom knew that even if you couldn't see it, there was blood on his hands. He'd killed a man.

He rushed to the fallen Warlock and pricked his finger with one of the shards of wood from the broken railing. He needed to do the right thing.

CHAPTER

THREE

TOM STARED into the eyes of a dead man. The man he'd murdered. He had hesitated too long and now it was too late to try to save him. A small part of his mind heard his name being called, but the sound seemed to be coming from far away.

His hand was still pressed against the Warlock's chest. The Warlock had placed his own hand over Tom's, clutching at it. Tom hoped it had given the man comfort as his heart ceased beating. The pressure should have stopped the bleeding if nothing else.

Why didn't I call 911? The Master...the man called for his Master's help, yet he did nothing. He even told me to kill him.

He felt a tug at his shoulder, insistent, urgent. A fist grasped his shirt and began to pull him. The Master was undoubtedly taking him away, to some secret lair, no doubt. Tom no longer had the heart to fight. He was a killer now and deserved his fate. Let The Master take whatever was left of Tom's soul, it no longer mattered. He knew at that moment he would never forgive himself.

A large hand spun him around where he met the anxious face of Headmaster Lianon. A wave of relief washed over Tom, and he fought a sudden urge to cry. The Headmaster would know what to do. He would know how to fix all of this. Maybe he could bring the Warlock to the Summer Iles and fix him, and Tom wouldn't have to live with the knowledge that he was a murderer. He gestured to the Warlock, trying to explain, but the words wouldn't come. He was so exhausted. Tom grabbed the Headmaster's sleeve, begging him to understand the silent plea for help, but the High Elf only shook his head.

"There's no time!" Lianon pulled on Tom's shirt, urging him to go with him.

Tom took a step and saw the ring, his father's ring, lying against the wall a short distance away. He tore away, lunging for it just in time. Lianon grabbed him with an iron grip. There would be no breaking away a second time. He shoved Tom through the Portal he'd created. The last thing he saw was a glimpse of The Master laughing, watching the whole thing as if it were a play being performed solely for his entertainment.

Tom landed in a heap on the carpet, the smell of a wood fire tickling his nose. He was safe in the Headmaster's office. The urge to cry was pounding at his sinuses and temples, but he fought against it as he tried to get up. Lianon extended a hand and Tom took it gratefully. He was led to a chair and a moment later, a blanket was draped over him. Though the room was warm, the weight of the blanket was comforting.

He focused on the fire quietly crackling to itself in the fireplace. It was warm and cheery. The Headmaster was on the phone with someone, Tom could hear in the background. But it was only noise, unimportant, and he couldn't follow the conversation anyway. In the flames, Tom saw the vacant, empty eyes of the dead Warlock and he couldn't look away. The tears broke free and ran hot down his cheeks. Breaths became sobs and they wracked his lungs with fear and anger and regret. He tried to remind himself that his family was safe, but at what cost?

A footman on silent feet appeared behind him as if formed by the smoke from the fire. He set a tray on the table between the armchairs and receded into the woodwork as unobtrusively as he'd arrived. The Headmaster came and sat as Tom lifted the delicate cup. It rattled on the saucer enough that the High Elf nearly reached to steady it, but Tom got the warm liquid to his lips and was able to take a sip. The welcomed warmth settled through his body, easing muscles he didn't realize were clenched. The warm brew seemed to steady him, calm him. Perhaps it was laced with some potion designed to do just that. If so, it was precisely what he needed right now and did not mind it.

"Before your mother and sister arrive," the Headmaster took a sip and continued, "let me apologize for taking so long to fetch you."

Not trusting himself yet, Tom swallowed the tea, ignoring the burn and letting the goodness wash through him. He placed the empty cup back on the tray before he broke the precious China. It had cracked under his strong, shaky grasp.

"I killed him." The words sounded unbelievable, unimaginable, even to him. Yet, he knew the truth of what he said, and it pained him more than he could express.

"I'm sure it was an accident. Self-defense, Tom." The slow, steady cadence of the words was infuriating and comforting at the same time. The Headmaster might have been talking about the weather for all the emotion he showed.

"I..." Tom needed to explain it to him, to make him understand, but it was impossible. Tom himself didn't understand. It was too strange, too foreign to even contemplate.

"Did he try to hurt you?" The Headmaster picked up his cup and regarded Tom over the brim. Tom nodded miserably. "Then it was clearly self-defense. I understand you're upset. A man died, but it was an unfortunate accident on your part." He took a sip to let that sink in. "Now, can you tell me what happened?"

The door swung open, and Tom jumped to his feet, fearing that The Master had somehow followed them. Though no one could breach The Academy, not even The Master. Instead, his mother and sister flew through the doorway, Lady Samsara sweeping in close on their heels.

Tom dropped back into his chair, the adrenaline charge spent, his heart racing.

"Tom, are you alright?" His mother fell to her knees beside him to embrace him in the chair. He hugged her back, but she pushed him back, her hands and eyes running through his hair, his arms, his chest. He realized she was trying to find out if he was hurt. Finding no injury, she held Tom's hand, her eyes questioning him.

"I'm unharmed," Tom said as he gently removed his hands from his mother's grasp and laid them palms down on his thighs. "I'm okay, really."

"The tea is hot," Headmaster Lianon waved to the tray by way of invitation. Tom did a double-take, there were suddenly three more cups and saucers waiting to be filled. Tabitha poured for herself and her mother as the Headmaster touched Lady Samsara's elbow. "Have you heard from Professor Thunderbolt?"

She nodded to the quiet question. "Yes, he's working with Head-mistress Clementine at Harding Academy. They took care of the... situation at the Callaghan home. The house has been put to rights, the wards are in place, but it's not safe for the family to go back there yet."

"I agree." The Headmaster himself poured her a cup and after a moment, he gently prodded Tom for the information again. "Tom was about to tell us what happened," he explained to the others.

"I killed him. That is, my blood killed him." A fresh tear followed the trails of his cheeks. Somehow, saying these words to his mother and sister made it all real in a way it hadn't been before. Confessing to them meant he couldn't deny it happened anymore. He wanted another cup of tea to soothe his throat, but the bile in his belly was looking for means of escape.

"Killed who?" Tabitha barely whispered the words, her eyes as wide as saucers.

Please, don't be afraid of me. He looked to his mother to judge her reaction. She was dabbing her eyes with a handkerchief, but her other hand was over her mouth. Tom couldn't handle the look in her eyes, mostly because he deserved it.

"I don't know," he answered his sister with honesty, as there was no hiding the details. They would all be known soon enough. "A Warlock. I don't...I don't know how. It was all...instinct...it happened so fast." He prodded the memory like an open wound trying to prize out bits and pieces of what happened. It was all a blur. He couldn't remember. Or maybe he did, but it wouldn't come to the surface of his mind, as a way of protecting himself? Was this a primal, survival way of keeping his sanity?

The Headmaster lay his hand heavily on Tom's shoulder, bringing him back to the present. "Take a breath. Start from the beginning. Tell us what happened after Arabella and Tabitha left with Professor Thunderbolt." His large hand gave him a reassuring squeeze. "I think we have all determined that what happened was an accident. No one is judging you and no judgment will be brought against you. That situation is handled. What we need from you now are the facts, so we know how to proceed."

Tom swallowed against the rising acid in his stomach and nodded. "After Mum and Tabitha left, I braced myself for a fight. I prayed reinforcements would come, but no one did." He felt a rising twinge of bitterness at that. *I was left alone to fight.*

"Why didn't you just summon a Door and leave?" asked Tabitha. "It's what I would have done. It's what any *sane* person would have done. You're just a lad. What did you think you could do against an army of Warlocks?"

Tom felt his hackles rise. She hadn't been there. She had no right to judge him. Hadn't the Headmaster just said so? The fact that she might have a point only made it worse. Tom clenched his teeth and tried to answer civilly. "There were wards on the house, and Thunderbolt said he'd be back with help. I thought I could hold down the fort until he came back. But he didn't." It felt a little wrong to blame someone else, especially someone who wasn't there to defend himself, but it was the truth.

"Anyway, the...The Master was there...and..."

"The Master?" His mother gasped. The look of pure fear in her eyes rattled him more than anything which had happened so far that night, except perhaps the vacant stare of the dead man.

"He took down the wards...a stream of Warlocks burst inside. I held them off as long as I could, but I guess The Master got impatient, and he came inside too." Tom stared down at his hands, seeing the Warlock's blood, a painful reminder of the day's outcome.

Lady Samsara refilled everyone's tea and fetched a wet towel for Tom's hands as though sensing his need to wash away what happened. "What happened then?" she asked.

Tom rubbed the cloth over his hands, but the memory of the blood was stubborn, refusing to budge long after his hands were cleaned. He scrubbed harder, digging into the flesh to wipe out what only he could see. His mother took the towel gently from him and held his hands as she gently took the cloth over his fingers and then kissed his forehead as though he were a child. "See?" She held up one hand, "All gone. All better." She made a show of throwing the towel in the fire and took a seat next to him.

"You know that suit of armor on the second floor?" Tom spoke to the flames. The burning cloth seemed to help somehow, as though the fall into ashes signaled the ordeal was finally over. "He animated it," Tom didn't wait for a response, the words just seemed to tumble from him now. "It attacked me. It spoke with his voice...I fought and fought...I didn't notice the Warlock who'd hidden in one of the rooms until it was almost too late."

Someone pressed the cup back into Tom's hand and he took a sip. His grasp was sturdier now, stronger. The dark tea barely shook this time. "I dodged his attack, but the armor cut my arm. I tossed it over the landing toward The Master. While I was distracted, the Warlock grabbed my wrist. I used the maneuver Master Smoke taught us in class: the push and twist. But my arm was bleeding really hard and as it shot out, the dripping blood morphed into a weapon." Hearing it back in a detached way like that made it sound ludicrous. Tom didn't expect anyone to believe him, he barely believed it himself.

"What do you mean, a weapon?" His mother's voice was nearly an octave higher and there was a note of panic behind the words.

Tom mimed the blood covering his hand and extending into a small spear. "I was going to push his arm down, but the...the blood extended past my hand, and it went right through him." He felt the tears reforming behind his eyes. He smiled in gratitude as Lady Samsara handed him a tissue. She followed that with a fresh cup of tea and the warmth centered him again.

"He fell to the floor and called The Master for help. All The Master did was egg me on to finish him off." Tom's bewilderment showed in the retelling. "I was...I was in a rage and to be honest..." he didn't want to say it, but he had to, "...I *did* consider it. I mean all these people ever did was put me, my family, and my friends in jeopardy. But I swear it was just a thought!" He fought to keep from wailing the last of the sentence but was only partly successful.

"Thoughts don't kill people, actions do." The Headmaster lay his hand gently on Tom's shoulder. "Anyone would have thought the same."

"I healed two people at Harding," Tom protested. "I was sure I could heal him, too, but I was afraid it might be a trap, and...and I hesitated. When I finally went to him, he was already dead. That's when the Headmaster arrived," Tom finished miserably.

In the silence that followed, the Headmaster shook his head and turned to Lady Samsara. "Please escort Tabitha and her mother to a room. They need rest. I'll escort Tom to his room and make sure he's settled." He took a deep breath before continuing. "We'll meet in the morning to decide on a course of action."

The women rose quietly. His mother seemed to be holding herself tightly, Tabitha just seemed in shock. They each gave Tom a fierce hug and neither of them appeared anxious to leave until Tabitha cleared her throat. His mother reached up to smooth a lock of hair from his face. "I...well...good night, Tom."

"Good night, Mum." Tom felt a little better. At least they weren't afraid of him, that was something. He watched them leave and stood a moment before heading to the door. He needed a shower and sleep. The weariness wore on him like a thick blanket.

"Just a moment, Tom," Lianon called from the desk.

"Sir, I'm exhausted."

"I know, Tom. And you are understandably distraught. But I must know the rest of the story." He gave Tom a knowing look.

"But Sir, I've told you everything. Did you not read my thoughts when we got back to school?" Tom assumed he had, though he wracked his tired mind for what the 'rest of the story' might be, but nothing came to him.

"Something's...changed, Tom. I cannot read your mind. Are you blocking me on purpose?"

"No, Sir!" Tom was appalled at the thought. "I would never do that." He paused for a moment as a new thought occurred to him. "Could you read my mind when we had our last chat?"

"Yes." The High Elf seemed lost in thought. When he continued, Tom wasn't sure if the Headmaster was talking to him or to himself. "So, it's a recent development. Perhaps your actions, though unintentional and regrettable, triggered another layer to your powers."

Tom deliberately opened his mind allowing the High Elf to enter, hoping, *praying* he would be able to read Tom's mind, that nothing had changed. "I'm scared, Sir."

Lianon looked up and smiled. It was a reassuring smile, one that warmed him with its kindness. "I know. Here, give me your hand if you like. You can send me your entire experience through touch." The Headmaster held out his hand and Tom took it. He had nothing to hide. There was a tiny spark, and his hand grew warm. The Headmaster nodded and said simply, "I see."

"I'm sure the teachers at Harding Academy can explain it better, but I have heard of blood weapons. It's meant as defensive magic wielded by Blood Mages, though no one has seen it used in...oh, hundreds of years." He looked as though he were reassessing Tom. "You've been wielding power from finite amounts of blood. I believe the injury you sustained was severe enough to trigger the defensive response. You were fighting off several attackers. Adrenaline was coursing through your veins. Your blood acted instinctively to protect you."

There were so many questions Tom wanted to ask, but as far as the blood weapon, even the Headmaster had confessed he didn't know much. Instead, Tom asked something else, something harder. "Sir, there are a few things I don't understand. Why and how did Professor Thunderbolt get into my room? He's not a Traveler, and besides, with the wards in place, no one but family should have been allowed in or out."

Professor Thunderbolt was, after all, a new teacher, and Tom knew very little about him.

"Lady Samsara opened a Portal for him." His warm face curled into a rueful smile. "I'm afraid Earthly magic is no match for High Elf magic. You may recall that she and I take turns overseeing the school. I was at the Summer Isles conferring with the council about your situation. Once she had dispatched Professor Thunderbolt, she reached out for me to come back to school. From inside your home, Professor Thunderbolt used a Door because he was with your mother and sister. Lady Samsara later sent him to Harding Academy to work on a solution with them. I came as soon as I found out."

"So, what now?" Tom asked quietly.

"Now, you get some rest. As I said, we'll make a plan in the morning." He sobered quickly and added, "I will not lie to you, Tom. I doubt The Master is done with you. Now that he's confirmed that you are, in fact, a Blood Mage, he will stop at nothing to get his hands on you and your power. Though he clearly has more knowledge than I do about what you are capable of, I believe you have the potential to be more powerful than even him. His purpose tonight was to manipulate you, scare you into submission while you are still somewhat manageable."

"And he almost succeeded. When I...when I killed the Warlock, I felt such utter despair that I would have gone with him." Tom spoke the confession so quietly that he barely heard it himself. Elven ears are sensitive and Lianon never missed a thing.

"I know." Lianon nodded, "I felt it too."

The old Headmaster's words sunk in slowly. He believed that Tom could defeat The Master? If he could, it would keep his family safe. If he had to kill to keep them safe...well, did it make sense to cry over a little spilled...blood? He opened his mouth to ask another question, but the Headmaster forestalled him by holding up a single hand. He led Tom from the office to the dormitories. They did not speak again until they entered Tom's room.

"You are safe here. Your mother and sister are safe. I know you feel terrible about the Warlock's death. I promise to ensure his loved ones are notified and taken care of," said the High Elf. "Get some rest. We'll talk in the morning."

"Thank you, Sir...for everything." Tom closed the door. Inexplicably, he felt better.

CHAPTER

FOUR

THE HALLWAYS ECHOED ALMOST HOLLOWLY, the quiet was a dramatic change from the talk and clatter when the students were milling around. With the denizens of the school off on holiday or spending Spring break with families, Tom was able to notice the compelling design of the building, the artwork that hung from the halls, all the details one missed while trying to dodge other students running from class to class. Tom found that he was starting to enjoy the simplicity of silence.

Needing a moment of solitude before he met with the others in the Dining Room, Tom headed for Lola's favorite bench behind the greenhouse. His mind was flooded with too many questions, and he needed to put some order to them.

What if The Master attacked again and managed to kidnap him? Would he take him or just his blood? What could The Master do if he had him? What else could be made if a weapon could be formed just from spilling his blood? How many lives would be in danger if he failed?

Tom sat with his hands resting on his thighs, breathing in for six counts, holding, then slowly exhaling to four counts. It was one of the breathing exercises that Professor Brambles had taught them, and he immediately felt better. He continued to breathe, clearing his mind until his inner world matched his peaceful surroundings.

Feeling somewhat better, he rose and headed to breakfast. It struck him that his life had been sheltered until recently. He'd been living in his own little bubble; safe, protected, and blissfully unaware of the evil that lurked in the world around him. Now, he felt...vulnerable.

As he entered the Dining Room, he saw his family and the Professors assembled at a table, relaxed, and enjoying each other's company, as if nothing had happened. It was as though The Master hadn't attacked with a swarm of Warlocks. As though Tom hadn't impaled a man with a weapon made from his blood.

Shaking off the thoughts, Tom offered a timid smile in greeting and kissed his mother's cheek. He extended a lame, "Good morning," to no one in particular, and went to fill his plate at the buffet.

The comforting aroma of bacon, eggs, sausage, fresh fruit, toast, and pastries filled his nose, as did the dark roasted aroma of coffee and the sweetness of fruit juices. Tom loaded his plate to the anticipation of his growling stomach. *When was the last time I ate?*

Tom sat with the others but ate in silence. He tried some of everything, from fruit to mounds of bacon and pancakes. Everything seemed to taste more sharply, like it was the first time he had tried each dish. He fell in love with food all over again.

"Using Blood Magick certainly creates an appetite, huh?" Tabitha chuckled, offering her brother a wink.

Tom smiled and wiped his mouth with his napkin. Tabitha no longer had the fearful look she had the night before. Seeing the color back in her cheeks, and the glint in her eye was reassuring. He'd understand if she was afraid of him, but that didn't mean he wanted her to be. She was his older sister, and he loved her dearly, despite a sometimes strained relationship where Tom occasionally thought Tabitha only cared for herself. The new softer side of her, Tom assumed, was purely due to her being terrified the night before. He didn't know how long this compassionate version of her would stick around, but that didn't matter just then. He was happy to see it. As much as he hated to admit it, shared trauma had a way of bringing people closer together.

"Tabitha!" His mother snapped the name and shot her daughter a strongly disapproving look.

"What? I'm just trying to lighten the atmosphere," Tabitha pushed a few crumbs around on her plate and rolled her eyes.

"This is no laughing matter!" Arabella sounded scandalized.

"It's fine, Mam, I don't mind." In fact, Tabitha gave Tom a sense of normalcy, something he desperately needed. He sat back and allowed his now full stomach a moment's rest. His pants felt tight around his waist, and he struggled to suppress a burp.

"Well, I do," Arabella fired back. She, at least, had not put it behind her.

"Tensions are still high," Thunderbolt temporized, "but I doubt Tabitha meant any harm."

Tabitha and Tom looked over to their mother, who fell into a sulky sort of silence and fiddled with her napkin. Tom's mother was a strong-willed woman and didn't like being told what to do or to be corrected by anyone. And to be called out in front of her children must be making her crazed.

No one said anything else until long after the table was cleared. Tom was bursting with questions, but under the circumstances, he didn't want to be the first one to speak. After the events of the previous day, he just wanted someone else to lead the conversation.

He had showered, slept, and eaten. His strength and energy were back, but his mind was still heavy. It suddenly occurred to him how much he missed small talk. *How is the weather? What are you planning for Spring break? Did you see the football match last night?* Apparently, no one else seemed inclined to talk about the minor things, so he sat and stared at the napkin twisting in his restless hands. He wished Lola and his friends were here. It was eery enough being in an empty school. Having a quiet breakfast with his mom and his Professors really wasn't his idea of a good time.

When the table was cleared and footmen vanished, the Headmaster turned to Tom's mother. "Is there somewhere you could go that would be safer than returning home?"

Arabella nodded thoughtfully. "Actually, we have several residences to choose from. I think...I think the London flat would be best. It's in the middle of a very busy neighborhood; any mischief there would be reported to the police immediately." She smiled at Lianon and added, "Despite how powerful The Master and his lot might be, they *are* still human and thus subject to human laws."

"Even so," Professor Thunderbolt looked thoughtful, as though he was working it out as he spoke, "I'll ask that wards be erected around the building. If, for some reason, you *must* leave the flat, do not go alone...and limit the number of staff members you employ. Stay with the ones you've known the longest and trust implicitly. If something feels off...anything at all...Travel back here or to another location."

Arabella nodded, but Tom could see in his mother's eyes that she believed all these precautions were unnecessary. As they rose to leave, Professor Thunderbolt took his leave. Lady Samara and Lianon walked with Tom and his family to the Main Hall. Tabitha summoned a Door and let her mother pass.

"Let me know if we can be of further assistance," Lady Samara called before leaving the Hall.

"I will inform you if there is any news," the Headmaster added.

Tom hesitated on the doorstep and turned back to the High Elf. "Thank you again, Sir. For...for everything," he said before closing the door quietly behind him.

CHAPTER

FIVE

THE WEALTH of a Traveler was passed down from generation to generation. Over the years, Tom's family had amassed properties in every major city: London, New York, Milan, Paris, and even more exotic locations. The London flat was one of the smaller, less assuming, homes they owned, but it was conveniently located.

"I always did love London," Tabitha said with a smile, plonking herself comfortably down on the large cream leather sofa.

There had been no time to call the Agency to stock supplies, but there were still water bottles in the kitchen. Since they were still sated from breakfast at the Academy, there would be time enough to see to such matters.

Tom settled more sedately in an armchair across from his sister with a cold bottle of water and settled in. His mother was pacing, as she said it helped her think. She was making a list out loud of necessities that needed to be brought in.

Tom shook his head at the size and scope of this list. "Mam, we're meant to be hiding out, not planning dinner parties."

"Just because we need to lie low, does not mean we have to live like heathens," his mother responded airily. Tabitha grinned at Tom and rolled her eyes.

"Headmaster Lianon advised against contacting friends and family while we're here. All it would take is one wrong word and a few loose lips, and The Master would know where we are again." The fact that Tabitha was lecturing their mother implied just how topsy-turvy everything had become; it was usually the other way around.

"I'm not dense, Tabitha. Surely there's nothing wrong with a phone call or text message?" Arabella sounded as exasperated as her daughter. Tom settled deeper into the cushions. It was because of him that they were all thrust together like this.

"Cell towers, Mam," Tabitha rolled her eyes, yet again. Tom wouldn't have been surprised if her eyes rolled right into her head. "We live in the twenty-first century."

That seemed to be the last straw. The two women began to argue, their volume increasing in an ever-growing demand to be heard over each other. Their argument reverberated off the walls and filled the room until Tom was sure there was no air remaining for him to breathe. Yes, they were both under a great deal of stress, but after all, it was *him* that The Master was after. So it was *him* who had to stand and fight The Master alone. And he did it to protect *them*. Maybe it was selfish, but it gnawed at him that no one thought about *his* stress, how *he* was taking being isolated from the world, hiding like a child.

"ENOUGH!" The sheer volume of Tom's outburst surprised even him. His mother and sister turned to him, eyes wide. He rose and confronted the two of them. "*I* am the Custodian. *I* am the man of the house. *I* will do what I must to keep us all safe." He shot his mother a hot glare. "Would you rather be a prisoner in a comfortable London flat with all your creature comforts or a prisoner of The Master and his band of minions?" Without waiting for an answer, Tom plowed over whatever his mother was trying to say. "I have enough to deal with right now without your bickering!"

Arabella gaped at him, eyes wide and mouth open, looking at all the world like a horrified fish. Tabitha giggled and grabbed her cellphone, snapping a picture of her mother's shock. Tom felt himself shaking slightly, surprised at his own temerity. He'd always been quiet, allowing others to speak over him, timid. *Where are these changes coming from?* Hormones? Was this the last gasp of adolescence? Was it something...deeper? Worse? Was it connected to using Blood Magick?

"I don't want to forget that look on her face," Tabitha grinned at her screen. She glanced at Tom and held up a hand for him to tap. "Respect, brother," she temporized.

"I'm tired," Tom mumbled under his breath. "I'm going to take a nap." He turned away from the hurt and shock on his mother's face. He no longer felt like a sixteen-year-old, but someone far older. Not wiser perhaps, but older. He closed the door to his room a bit more forcefully than he needed to, but the loud SNAP felt satisfying.

His room had been undisturbed since the last time they were in London. And though he had changed so much since that time, most notably in the past twelve hours, it still felt comfortable. He threw himself on the familiar bed and only then remembered how good that mattress felt, soft and yielding. The memory foam eased under his aches and pains, and he slipped easily into a deep sleep.

He woke several hours later, splashed water on his face, and made his way back downstairs. His mother was unpacking cartons of food from a delivery service. "Ah, Tom." She smiled and handed him a box. "Just in time to help me put these away."

Tom suppressed a yawn and only glanced at the food as she handed it to him. The refrigerator was comfortably stuffed. "Look," he held up the container and stopped her for a moment, "I'm...I'm sorry for snapping earlier, I was tired and stressed. And...to be honest...I don't know where these sudden fits of anger are coming from."

Arabella closed her hand around his, the box of frozen lasagna dangling between them. "Tom, after all you've been through, it's no surprise that you're feeling that way. Anyone would be on edge after having gone through half of what you've had to endure."

She let go and gestured for him to put the food in the freezer. "To be honest, that's probably what set off your sister and me. We had only worried about you and we still were so stressed, that...well, we took it out on each other. I don't think Tabitha is quite over her own ordeal. I know I'm not."

A momentary surge of displeasure went through him. Okay,

Tabitha had been kidnapped and injured. And his mom had to live through the trauma of having another of her children attacked by a madman. But how did that compare to what he was going through? He had killed a man...

Tom fought that line of thinking into submission and ground it under his heel. It wasn't worthy of him and frankly, that way of thinking was foreign to him. She was right, of course, if the situation was reversed, he would have been a nervous wreck.

He put the food away and leaned against the refrigerator. He found himself asking the question that had been burning in the back of his mind. "What I don't understand..." he paused, trying to put his thoughts into words and then get them organized. "Surely The Master didn't expect me to rush to his side and call him 'Master'."

The image of the dying Warlock calling out "Master, help me!" intruded his thoughts. He pushed it away. "I mean..." he forced the words out as if their very presence could distance himself from the memory. "What purpose was served in attacking me? Was he testing my powers? I had already turned Jameson down. He had to know I would put up a fight. Jameson said they needed my *blood*? Is the Magick a by-product of my blood and not me? If he drained me, could he use it for himself?"

Arabella grabbed his arms and turned him to her. She looked into his eyes and Tom was startled. Somehow, he'd gotten much taller than she was. When did that happen? "Listen to me. You have power. According to the Headmaster, it's..." she paused, and Tom realized she was searching for a word, a *safe* word.

"...frightening?" He offered the word. Maybe there was an edge to it. He had been so sure that his mother and sister were no longer afraid of him, and now he wondered. It wasn't fair. After all, it wasn't *his* fault he had Blood Magick.

"I was going to say that any power is irresistible to some people. Evil men with power will always want more."

Tom blushed, not at her words, but because he had been so quick to take offense where there was none. "That still doesn't answer my question," he reminded her.

"Tom." Arabella let him go, but she held his gaze. "I'm your mother. I've seen you with scraped knees, cuts, and bloody lips. Your blood has never...well..." she swallowed, "never behaved differently than anyone else's blood. It's *you* he wants."

"But...why attack me? I mean...I need to know what he's after if I'm going to fight him."

Arabella looked at him as if he'd just declared he was a fish. Then she barked a short, derisive laugh that she couldn't stop. "Simple." She shook her finger in his face. "You're *not*. You're going to leave this to the Headmaster and that Professor Thunderbolt. *You* are going to hide out here just like they told you to."

"But..."

"No buts, Tom. No."

"But Headmaster said that I was stronger than The Master..."

"He did *not*." Arabella was flushed now, the blood running to her cheeks, her eyes boring into Tom's. "He said you MIGHT. MIGHT. BECOME. Might Become. *Someday*. Not now. That evil man has *years* of experience on you and he's merciless. You yourself told me he just threw away the life of one of his followers, and for no reason."

Tom opened his mouth to object, but there was nothing he could say to that. He might be more powerful than The Master, but that didn't mean he was stronger. Still, digging into the London house and hiding under a blanket like a terrified little boy grated on him.

"I should still have a say in what..."

"Thomas." Arabella called him that when he was in trouble, or when she thought he was. "You will stay out of this. Completely. NO BUTS!" she stopped him before he could speak. "Period. End of discussion. Your sister and I must wait here and so do you. Understood?"

Tom bristled, but he swallowed what he was going to say and instead nodded miserably.

CHAPTER
SIX

THE HALLS once more echoed with the sounds of students running to and from classrooms. After seeing them empty the last time he was at the school, Tom was taken aback for a moment by the noise and the pressing of the crowd. It didn't take long, however, for him to acclimate to the old school. At the same time, Tom wondered if he'd ever truly fit it anywhere now that he was so different.

Studying the same old subjects while a powerful, evil Sorcerer was hunting you and your family made it difficult to concentrate. It all seemed pointless, ridiculous even, and Tom found his mind wandering. He was anxious to return to his *new* school. While they had much of the same curriculum, they had more...practical studies as well. He missed his private lessons with Professor Montague. That was the only time he felt empowered.

At least until he went back, he had Lola and Devlin to rely on. He found his friends at lunch and Lola rose to give him a hug. Devlin punched his shoulder and pointed to an empty chair. "We didn't know if you were here or not, but we saved you a seat."

Tom grinned and half fell into the chair. "I take it you heard?"

"You're lucky he didn't kill you," Lola said without preamble. Tom felt his hackles rise. Like all his accomplishments, all the fighting he'd done counted for nothing? It was all luck? Before he could speak, Devlin jumped in.

"Heard you took him on by yourself." He looked impressed and Tom felt a little better, though Lola's comment still rankled.

"I was the only one there..." he tried to be modest about it, but truthfully, he was feeling proud of himself. He shrugged as self-effacing as he could.

"You shouldn't have been," Lola insisted. "Why did you stay and fight? You should have run when you had the chance."

"I survived, didn't I?" Tom snapped at her.

She retreated, but she cast a look at Devin for support. Were they talking about him telepathically? Playing good cop, bad cop? Micro-managing him? Lola was starting to sound like his mother and not his...well, girlfriend. "Besides, I was defending my family."

Devlin nodded. "I understand. It is your duty as Custodian." Tom felt validated. Devlin got it.

"Well, I don't." Lola hissed at Devlin. "What I heard was that your Mom and Tabitha were evacuated, but you stayed to fight."

"It wasn't like that." Tom felt his ire rising. Why couldn't she just drop this?

"Tom," Devlin broke in again. "Tell us what it was like. All we heard was that you fought, but we haven't heard much else."

Tom glanced over his shoulder. He wasn't chomping at the bit to share the tale, even with his closest friends. But for all her nagging, Lola loved him and only wanted him to be safe. And Devlin would have his back, no matter what. He took a breath and replied, "Not here."

They reconvened at the Meditation platform. Tom started at the beginning but skipped the part where he killed the Warlock. They didn't need to know about that, and the Headmaster had cautioned him to not reveal that portion of his abilities, at least not until Tom had a better handle on them.

He skipped the retrieval of the signet ring as well, as he would have had to admit where it had gone and how it was retrieved. Besides, it was hardly important, was it? He had the ring back, that's all that mattered. Though Lola and Devlin were new Travelers, they both gasped when he told them how the Master had stolen his Key. Tom rushed through the rest of the tale, finishing with how he rejoined his mother and sister at the school. He was vague when recounting how he spent Spring break, merely saying he and his family had been Traveling. He hated keeping secrets from his friends, but recent events were making him paranoid. He still couldn't shake the idea that there might be a mole in their midst.

When he finished, Devlin let out a low whistle. "That is..." he shook his head in disbelief. "You actually faced him down, I mean mano-a-mano." He nodded toward Lola. "She's right, you know, you *are* lucky to be alive."

Tom felt an annoyance at his words, but it didn't raise his hackles as Lola had. After reciting the events once more, he secretly agreed with Devlin. He *was* lucky to be alive. For that matter, *why* was he alive? The Master could have finished him off while he was kneeling over the dead Warlock. The Headmaster had pulled Tom away. If High Elf magic was stronger than Earthly magic, why didn't the Headmaster fight The Master? At the very least, they could have captured and questioned him. Surely the Council of Earthly Magical Beings would agree it was a safe course of action.

"Tom?" Lola spoke softly. Tom shook himself out of the reverie. There were so many questions from that night, so many things left unexplained. They would have to be answered later.

Right. I'll just find The Master and ask him.

"Sorry, I was lost in thought. I mean...I'm just supposed to go back to classes when there's a maniac on the loose. I'm supposed to focus on...," he waved at the school bag he'd flung onto the platform, "...*books*? What I need is training and experimentation to find out what I *can* do and how to protect my mother and sister."

"You'll protect them by staying out of sight." Lola lay her hand on his arm. His irritation with her had returned and her touch was itching, annoying even.

"Ok, fine. Whatever, I just...I think I deserve to know what the plan is, or even if there is one."

"Why? The Headmaster and the Professors have years of experience and Elf magic is a lot stronger..."

"...than human." Tom finished sharply. "I know, I have been told over and over how powerful it is, but he didn't face The Master did he? And if Professor Thunderbolt was so great, how come he wasn't there either?" He clenched his fists and paced with the frustration of trying to explain himself. "You don't understand. I have to protect my family, *me*. I have that responsibility, *I* have the responsibility to keep them safe and they're only in danger because of *me*!" He stopped, realizing he was getting louder and louder. He took a breath and continued in a softer tone. "I should at least get some say in my future."

"Tom," Lola said as though she were explaining something to an oblivious child. "It's just that I'm scared for you. Taking on The Master? If even Lianon won't do that, what chance do you have?"

"Maybe I'm stronger than he is." Tom spat back at her. She sighed and he knew he should stop there, but Tom's back was up. "The Headmaster said that I was, or that I could be, at any rate." He turned away from her and faced Devlin. "And you? Are you on her side?"

"There's no *side*!" Lola objected, slapping her palm down on her thigh in annoyance.

"Tom, just lay low for a while. You and Tabitha are safe here at The Academy. I'm sure they have someone watching over your mother while you're here."

"Safe?" Tom echoed Devlin. "Safe, like a bug hiding under a rock. Safe until we come out, until we let our guard down. The house was protected with layers upon layer of wards, yet The Master still breached them. My Mam is moving around every other day, never staying in one spot too long. What kind of life is that for her? Always looking over her shoulder, having to trust people to keep her safe? Where was the vaunted Elf magic when I needed it yesterday?" He found himself breathing rapidly. "What I *need* is training. I need to get stronger, reach the 'untapped' power." He used air quotes and the word came out bitter and harsh.

"Until then," Devlin said reasonably, "maybe you should..."

"Maybe." Tom spoke over him, no longer concerned about volume,

"Maybe I should go back to Harding Academy and study something important! Not just on Saturdays, but full time."

"You mean study with someone like Zaina?" Lola said in a dangerous whisper.

A part of Tom's mind warned him that he was on thin ice, but he ignored it. He stared at Lola, trying to understand the change in subject. He shrugged, confused, and Lola's face grew white with anger.

"Idiot!" She spun on her heels and stormed off.

"What was that about?" Tom turned to Devlin.

"Jealousy, betrayal, hormones," Devlin said. "Take your pick." He grabbed his books and followed in Lola's wake.

Tom sat on the platform, trying to understand what just happened. It didn't matter. Not with The Master after him and his family. Whatever that was all about with Lola and Devlin, that was something for him to take care of later. After he defeated The Master.

Because he would have to, wouldn't he? So far, he hadn't seen anyone with enough power to even touch what he'd seen The Master do that night.

He allowed himself a moment, daydreaming of The Master fallen at his feet. Maybe another blood spear? The memory brought him back as quickly as a face full of cold water. No. He didn't want to kill. Not again. Never again.

But is there any other way to make sure The Master won't come after him and those he loved?

There had to be a way. He needed more information and he needed to be stronger. Much stronger. Stronger than Lianon. Stronger than The Master.

And if that meant The Master had to die, it would likely be up to him, wouldn't it? It wasn't Tom's fault that his adversary didn't know when to back down. It wasn't just his friends and family. If the Master had his way, the whole world was in jeopardy.

CHAPTER

SEVEN

TOM FOUND HIMSELF ALONE. This was becoming more and more common of late. Even his Saturday classes had been cut short. Until Lianon cleared him to return to Harding, Tom went to school, then back to the ward-protected London flat on the weekends. And now for Spring break. How safe that was, Tom couldn't be certain. The Master had broken through the wards guarding their other house without too much effort. Still, when he was home, he could check on his mother, and he would know where Tabitha was. No weekend trips with friends for any of them.

He and Tabitha saw their friends at school during the week. If their mother was following the rules, her weeks must be terribly boring, stuck within the walls of their apartment. For months, she'd been without a Key, and now that it had been returned, she could only move from home to home. The forced isolation was driving her mad and, therefore, she apparently thought it was her duty to make everyone else mad too.

With Lola and Devlin inexplicably giving him the cold shoulder, there was no one to speak to at school, not really. So, he attended classes, trying to politely pretend to pay attention to macroeconomics, and the political unrest in the Middle East while formulating plans to take out The Master in his mind. It was a waste of time, but time was what he had in abundance. The only one who knew when The Master would strike next was The Master. So, Tom went through the motions of living and chafed that he wasn't being more proactive.

When he went home, he isolated himself in his room, mindlessly fiddling with the signet ring. It had become a habit as though he were trying to find the right combination to hang on his finger. Even the ring didn't feel right anymore, as if the very bedrock of everything he used to be had been shattered in that one night. In some ways, his own skin no longer fit properly, giving him a restlessness that could not be satisfied by the mundane actions of everyday life. He ate with his family, but in the end, he preferred to be alone, at least for now.

It had been weeks since the battle with The Master and so far, he hadn't heard a thing from anyone. If anything official had been decided, no one had told him. His mother and sister did their own thing, and never discussed the reason why they were spending so much time as a family. And his friends, well, they remained polite but aloof. He wasn't ready to call them "former friends." Not yet. Even the Headmaster seemed to be keeping his distance. Tom hadn't seen much of him at all. Meanwhile, The Master was still out there, hatching evil plans.

He told himself that a little separation from Devlin and Lola was likely for the best. Friends of his were automatically put in the line of fire. If his family was targeted for his sake, then friends were likewise just as vulnerable. He used that as reassurance when he felt isolated or alone.

Like now. Lying on his bed, he tried to disappear into his head-phones. He turned the volume up to vanish into the music, but it occurred to him that he wouldn't be able to hear if an alarm sounded or if someone screamed for him to save them. In the end, he settled for listening through a single earbud just to remain vigilant.

After the second day of self-imposed isolation, he began to wonder what he could learn on his own. Whether it was him or the blood, the Magick was at hand. If no one was going to get him ready to battle The Master, then maybe he needed to find other ways to prepare.

If no one had said anything about training or teaching him how to defend himself thus far, then they likely wouldn't. The fact that he kept hearing repeatedly how the "adults" should handle everything, and he should hide under the bed until they did, rather proved that point. They were deliberately holding him back when he was very nearly an adult himself. To him, it didn't begin to make sense. Especially since before things came to a head with the Master, all his mentors were keen on helping him to develop his abilities.

Who had fought The Master? Tom did. Professor Thunderbolt had run off. Sure, he took Tom's family to safety, but he hadn't come back, had he? And Lianon? The old High Elf had practically grabbed Tom and thrown him through a Portal like he was pulling a child from a burning building. He didn't actually *fight* The Master, did he?

So how was Tom supposed to leave the battle to the very people that refused to fight in the first place? Running away wasn't the answer. Cowering in a house entrusted to wards that had already failed once made no sense either.

The answer was simple. Power. If Tom was...*eventually*, he sneered at the word, destined to defeat his enemy, then it was high time he learned how. He threw the Economics book across the room in frustration. It really wasn't *fair*. It was Tom whom The Master was tracking. It was Tom who put his family and friends at risk. For whatever reason The Master wanted him. Why shouldn't it be Tom who fought him? It should have been obvious, but instead, everyone held him down, kept him back.

The Master isn't waiting. He's gathering his strength. He's replacing his minions. A familiar surge of guilt came with that thought, but Tom fought it down.

"Tom?" His mother knocked on his door. "Is everything alright?"

"Yes." *No, nothing is all right.* "I just dropped a book."

"From how high up?" His mother asked, but he suspected he wasn't supposed to hear that, given she was already walking away.

He stood and began pacing the room. It was like he had too much energy and he had to do *something*. But since he wasn't allowed to do anything *useful*, he might as well pace in the prison cell of his room.

If he were honest with himself, getting away last time *was* lucky. Lola was right about that, at least. But The Master wasn't stupid. He would be ready next time. He wouldn't let Tom get away again.

He twisted the ring on his finger again, something to keep his hand busy while he thought. *He won't let me get away again.* The thought ran through his head like it was on repeat. There was something in there that sounded important. He snorted and twisted the ring hard enough to feel the friction on his finger. *Of course it's important. It's frightening.*

Tom ran his fingers along the spines of the books in his bookcase, recalling the battle absently.

He'd hesitated. True, he'd hesitated to help the injured Warlock. But when Lianon opened a Portal and called for him...several times... Tom had hesitated. He'd killed a man and he was staring over the corpse in disbelief. Lianon had called him more than once. Tom had been open, exposed, vulnerable.

Lianon was powerful and it was likely true that Elven magic was stronger than human, but something wasn't clicking. The Headmaster hadn't attacked, he hadn't thrown any spell at The Master, he'd only dragged Tom through the Portal...*after* Tom dithered and waited and tried to understand what it was that had happened to him.

How was it they had gotten away?

"Finish him," was all The Master said and waited...he *waited* for Tom to finish him instead of pressing the advantage and taking Tom. It made no sense. If he...

"Ouch." Tom looked down at the signet ring. All of his twisting and messing with it had caused a bit of loose skin at the base of his finger to catch and pinch. He held that finger in his other hand until the sharpness went away, glad for the pain, which had brought him so sharply back to what was right in front of his face.

He'd been thinking long enough. It was time to do some experimenting on his own. If no one was going to teach him about Blood Magick, then he'd teach himself.

CHAPTER

EIGHT

"IT'S NOT FAIR." Tom stood in front of Headmaster Lianon's desk. He had been trying to get the High Elf to understand, to explain to him how it felt to be so helpless, but it seemed like Lianon wasn't listening. Worse, he wasn't going to listen, no matter what Tom said. "I mean, with all due respect, Sir, and I mean that, in the end, this is my fight."

"Tom, I understand your frustrations…"

The Headmaster spoke patiently, though a vocal part of Tom's mind doubted it. He couldn't *really* know. How could he? When was *he* ever stalked, or *his* family used against him?

"But this is something you can't simply barrel into. 'The Master,' as he styles himself, is too powerful. The safest thing to do is wait."

"But…Sir, what is it exactly we're waiting for? I mean, unless you think he's going to change his mind and leave me alone…"

"I seriously doubt that." The Headmaster shook his head.

Tom just knew what was coming next. He could almost recite it by heart by now: *powerful, relentless, wants your ability…blah, blah, blah…*

"Then what purpose does it serve to wait?" Tom asked, trying hard to be reasonable.

But Lianon seemed set on being irritating. For the life of him, Tom couldn't figure out why he should tie himself up in knots over a basic question. The frustration had taken hold of him, and he couldn't stop himself.

"You need to be more powerful, more *controlled*..." Lianon slammed his hands on the desk, leaning on them as he spoke. As if by somehow closing the gap between them, he could force Tom to see things his way.

It should have been a warning, but Tom simply talked over him. "How can I get stronger by staying here? How am I supposed to learn *control* if there is no one to teach me? I was supposed to be at Harding on Saturdays. In the meantime, while we hide away here like cockroaches under the carpet, *HE* is getting stronger, and my family remains unprotected!"

"Your sister is right here during the week, with you. Besides, there are new wards around..."

"Wards?" Tom hadn't meant to shout the words, but it was just so ridiculous. "He cut through the wards like they didn't exist. They're nothing to him!"

"Tom..."

"And while we're sitting here doing nothing, what is *he* doing?"

"Tom!" The Headmaster drew himself up to new heights.

"What does he want from me!?" Tom reached up and wrapped his fist in his hair. He was hardly able to restrain himself from pulling it out. The pain of yanking it cut through the anger and helped to ground him. Still, he couldn't stop the frustration from coming, it had been too long buried. "Blood!? He can have it. I'll give him a quart. I only need a drop to take him down. Heck, I'll even donate it if it brings him out to where we can get him!"

"THOMAS!" Lianon slammed a fist on the desk. A framed photo jumped and fell, the sound of glass fracturing echoed in the silence. Tom marshaled himself, shoving down the anger that had been building. To his horror, he belatedly realized that he had been screaming at the Headmaster of the school.

"I'm..."

Sorry. I'm sorry. Just say the word. Say it out loud.

Headmaster Lianon stepped back from the desk. He let out a

breath, his shoulders losing some of their stiffness. "Tom." He might have been calmer, but he still spoke as though Tom were a petulant child, the single word slipping out of his mouth almost as a sigh. That too was annoying, but Tom had to admit that it was justified. Maybe he did sound like a child throwing a temper tantrum, but the High Elf had no reason to patronize him. If he'd considered Tom an adult in the first place, he never would have lost his temper.

Tom reached over to the desk and righted the picture. "I should clean that up for you..."

Liannon started to say something, but a shard sliced Tom's finger. Tom stuck the injured digit in his mouth. *Great, I'm trying to convince him I'm an adult by having a temper tantrum and now I'm sucking my fingers.*

"Tom. I know that I am asking a lot of you, but there is more support than just Professor Thunderbolt and myself behind you. I have been enlisting help from other places, talking to others to understand what we are up against. And please believe me when I say that *we* are up against this, not just you."

Tom pulled the finger from his mouth and pressed his thumb against the nick, trying to force the bleeding to stop without healing it. He felt perverse regarding that part of himself right now. "I need training anyway...Sir." He was proud of the way he had his voice under control again. "Why not start there?"

"I do agree that you should go back to Harding." Lianon sank slowly into his chair again. "We've had to wait until they improved their protections and security, but I believe they are ready for you now, if you want to go. They have better facilities for what you need." If he was put out by this admission, he didn't show it.

"Thank you, Sir." It wasn't all Tom had wanted, but it was a start. "As soon as I return from the class trip, I will make arrangements."

Lianon shifted in his chair and made a grimace. "As far as that goes...I've cleared it with your Professors, and we have determined that going on an international class trip would not be wise."

"But..." Tom forgot about the cut and stood staring dumbfounded at the Headmaster. "It's for Middle Eastern Studies. It's for my major. That trip is half of the grade for the semester."

The High Elf was already nodding. "Yes, I realize this. And I am sorry, but it's simply too dangerous right now. There is no way to protect you on such a trip. You must see that."

"So, I fail the class?"

"No. As I said, I have spoken to your Professors, and we have agreed to allow you to make up the assignment in the library here. A paper..."

"It's part of my *Global Studies Major!*" Tom emphasized the words in case the old man didn't understand. In order to study the world, one had to go out *into* the world. "I can't learn what it feels like in...in...in Abu Dhabi from a book. I can't experience the Wailing Wall from some second-hand report and a handful of photographs and some video footage from someone else's trip!"

"I'm afraid it's the best we can do under the circumstances."

"So..." Tom's thumb was pressing hard on the cut now. He could feel the edges of it coming together, healing despite himself. The newfound restraint was eroding beneath him, but the unfairness of the past few days was killing him. "So, a crazed Warlock attacks me and *I'm* the one that has to suffer for it? Why isn't The Master paying for all he did? Why am I the one that gets to have his life completely overturned?"

"Tom..." it was as weary as Tom had ever heard the old High Elf.

"You're afraid of him." He made this an accusation, intending to hurt the Elf, to rile him into action.

"Yes," the Headmaster admitted. "I am.

The quiet answer left Tom off-balance. For a moment he gaped at the Headmaster, not sure he was hearing correctly.

Lianon drew himself up, a soldier already weary from battle but carrying on anyway. "So would any intelligent person. So should you be. And that is what I have been wanting you to understand. You need to be afraid, Tom."

"I fought him once," Tom said without heat. Even he wasn't stupid enough to think he'd won.

But he hadn't exactly lost, either.

"No, Tom. You didn't." The Headmaster's voice could have frozen helium. "You fought his minions. While he watched. It was a test, Tom. He wanted to see what you were capable of."

"But the armor…"

"You yourself said you were distracted. The automaton had a clear shot and what did it do? Cut your arm. It could have *killed* you, but all it did was make you bleed. It wasn't a fight, Tom, it was a test. You performed for him. You didn't fight him. And that Warlock you killed? He *merely grabbed your arm*, Tom. Even that wasn't a magical fight. You didn't beat him. You told The Master everything he wanted to know about you."

Tom felt a rock form in his stomach. Was that true? Had The Master played him for a fool?

Of course he did. I am a fool.

But then, wasn't the Headmaster playing Tom for a fool too, by not letting him train?

He looked down at the drop of blood on his finger. It glistened in the light and left a narrow red trail as it pooled and slid down his hand. For a lingering moment, the office he was standing in took on a brighter image. The books on the shelves, instead of being nondescript identical bindings, showed in brilliant color and he could guess what each one contained in their pages just by glancing at them. He also realized how easily those pages could burn. The shining desk was little more than splinters that had yet to be separated but could easily be allowed to shatter. The glass in the windows ached to burst open and the entire world seemed to be poised, breathless, waiting for Tom's pleasure.

Tom swallowed hard and reminded himself to breathe.

"It's not fair," Tom whispered to the drop of blood as it disappeared into his finger, the wound finally closing, despite himself. "It's not fair."

CHAPTER
NINE

"IT'S NOT FAIR." Tom leaned back against the wall, one foot on the bench where Zaina and Mandy were sitting and watching him. It was Friday afternoon. He'd been back at Harding for all of an hour and already he felt more at home than he had all week at The Academy.

"Nope." Benny shook his head. He was standing next to Tom, a trash can between them like a stunted guard. "It's not fair at all. I mean 'let us handle it' is fine and all, but then they *don't* handle it."

"Exactly!" Tom jumped on that. "Either show me how or get it done, or...something. Anything. All they're doing now is...nothing." He threw his arms up in disgust. "How can you see what that maniac did and know that people are in danger and do...nothing?"

"Maybe they *are* doing something," Mandy offered, always the one to try and see the bright side of things. "Maybe they're just not including you with what they're doing?"

"That's just as bad," Zaina shook her head emphatically. "Maybe even worse." She gestured at Tom. "It's his life at risk, it's his family at stake. They shouldn't do a thing without telling him."

"Yes!" Tom felt vindicated. "Exactly!"

"Telling him?" Benny scoffed. "He should be asked, like for permission." He shrugged.

Tom tried to imagine Headmaster Lianon asking Tom for permission and failed. He didn't think it had to go that far. He didn't need to give *permission*, he just wanted to be included in the plans. He said nothing, though. After being treated like an errant child, being informed was at least a step in the right direction. He fantasized that he could be magnanimous and allow the Headmaster leeway, allowing him to make his own decision so long as Tom was kept in the loop. And trained.

At least he'd finally been allowed back to weekend classes at Harding. It was a step in the right direction. Somewhat. But could a few hours every Saturday possibly be enough to give him the control he so desperately needed over his Blood Magick?

Still...was there *anyone* else that had a chance against The Master? Lianon's words echoed in the back of his mind, and truth be told, they had never stopped. "...stronger than The Master..."

"Tom?" Zaina called impatiently. Shaking off his fantasy, Tom realized he'd not been paying attention to the discussion.

"I'm, sorry." He offered his friends an apologetic smile. "It's just that everyone seems to be wanting me to run and hide and allow other people to fight for me."

"Who?" Zaina asked, her nose wrinkling as she frowned.

Tom shrugged. "They keep saying to let Headmaster Lianon and Professor..."

"No." Zaina interrupted, with an impatient shake of her head. "I mean, who's been saying that to you?"

"Oh. Well, the Headmaster, and Professor Thunderbolt, of course."

"Of course," Benny echoed, the chubby boy's tone was mocking. "Naturally, *they* would."

"My mother and sister," Tom added, the frustration he'd been bottling up bubbled slowly to the surface. His friends, his *new* friends nodded as if that was little surprise. "...people at school..."

"Wait." Zaina raised her hand to stop him from going further. "Your friends are telling you to run and hide?"

"Don't they understand the stakes?" Benny sounded affronted. "I mean it's not *their* families at risk."

"Okay," even the placid Mandy seemed a bit put off by this, "I agree that you need to be told what's going on and what they're planning, I just don't think you need to run off and fight him again. Remember David and Goliath? It's not always the strongest who wins. Sometimes it's the most devious, and from what I understand, The Master is as evil as they come."

After a moment of silence, Zaina grinned at the girl. "I think that's the longest sentence I ever heard you speak." Mandy shot her a sour look, but a slight blush on her cheeks belied any ill feelings.

"I just think...you need to understand the power you *do* have, and you might not need to be stronger, just...I don't know...wiser?" She waved her hands as if she were trying to capture the right words.

Tom fought his initial defensiveness. Mandy wasn't against him. She wasn't telling him to let others fight his fights for him. She was merely pointing out the same lament Tom had been ruminating on since that fateful day when The Master defeated the wards. "I *know* that." He held up a hand in apology when Mandy flinched. "Sorry, it's just so frustrating. I've been asking for training, for someone to show me what I am capable of, and no one will."

Benny barked a laugh. "They probably can't, bro. No one else has what you've got. I've never seen or even heard of anyone that works Blood Magick outside of the history books. And even those don't give many details."

"Yeah," Tom acknowledged that, but it wasn't the first time he'd considered it. "And I realize I'm not the first, but it's been a while. I mean, there haven't been any Blood Mages for hundreds of years or whatever. History books aren't giving us what we need. More often than not, they leave out the details of what really went on. Maybe another kind of book? Some sort of memoir maybe? A journal at the very least? There's got to be something in the archives. *Something.* As far as I can tell, no one has even been looking."

"Then do it yourself," Zaina said reasonably.

Tom blinked. "What do you mean?" he asked, wondering if she was suggesting what he thought she was.

"I mean, if no one will teach you, then it's time to be self-taught.

Experiment, see what you can learn on your own." She waited while Tom considered that and then continued cajoling. "What harm could it do? It's just a finger prick and drop of blood."

Not even that, with his healing power. But he got the point she was making.

"I..." Tom thought about it carefully. The frustration seemed to be lessening. He could think again. This was the big difference being with friends who supported you and believed in you. Interested now, and feeling better than he had in ages, he sat up and considered his hands. "How would I start?"

"Prick your finger?" Benny suggested with a smirk.

Tom slugged his shoulder. "I know that much, I mean, what do I do? A spell? Are there words to say? Hand gestures? What do I try?"

"Well, you said that the suit of armor attacked you?" Mandy asked. Tom nodded. "Start there."

"You have a suit of armor handy?" Benny laughed.

Zaina glared. "I mean, try to animate something. Like a statue or fling a rock or something."

"Yeah." Tom nodded. He felt better than he had in some time. Was it possible to teach himself and be good enough to defend his family the next time The Master showed up? He told himself that even bad training was preferable to no training at all, and that seemed to be an alternative. Besides, he was only tossing a rock. If it was done somewhere kind of deserted, no one would even know.

"Alright." Tom straightened up and rubbed his hands together. "Let's find a rock and someplace where no one will see."

"There's the garden shed." Zaina thought for a moment. "It's made of brick, so throwing a few rocks wouldn't hurt it. There's at least one wall without any windows, and it's set away from the rest of the campus."

Benny stared at her. "I didn't know there was a garden shed. Why not go to the Eastern Tower?"

"The Tower's a known hangout. The shed is impossible to see from the school. It's perfect." Mandy grinned. "Us girls went exploring one day and found it kind of by accident."

"Let's go." Zaina rose from the bench like a silken mist. Tom enjoyed watching her move, she had the grace of a swan. For a moment he was surprised. Since Lola had come into his life, he hadn't noticed the first thing about any other girls. Yet there was something about Zaina that drew the eye.

Which drew him.

He coughed, using the gesture to shake the weirdness of feeling any of that. "All of us?" Tom looked from her to Benny to Mandy as he realized suddenly what they were saying. He hadn't expected to have such a wide audience.

"Why not?" Benny walked over to where Zaina was waiting, Mandy jumped up to follow.

"But...don't you have classes? Don't you have Divination or something after lunch?"

Benny shook his head. "Will you listen to yourself? You've been complaining that you can't get training and now you're stalling? Divination! If you must know, we have Study Hall on Friday afternoons. Let's just say that we've decided to study Blood Magick today. Come on." He waved Tom forward into the quad, ignoring the fact that Tilly, the young Witch who oversaw Study Hall would mark them absent and they would likely get into trouble.

Tom followed along behind the others, uncomfortable with the speed of the decision. Of course, Benny was right. He couldn't very well complain that no one was doing anything and then refuse to participate when someone offered to help. That was just a different way of letting others take on his battles for him and he was tired of that already. Besides, what difference was it to him if some of his friends cut class to be with him? In a way, it was kind of nice. A show of solidarity, which had been lacking back at The Academy.

The shed turned out to be perfect. It had been a sort of carriage house or something back in the day. It was a brick edifice, though it had a window on one side opposite the door. The whole building was covered by ivy left untended through years of neglect. Even the tools inside were almost completely covered with dead leaves and scattered refuse.

It was on the far side of the school grounds. Tucked away from the quad, hidden behind a copse of trees that gathered around, branches intertwined in a frozen dance, a large uninterrupted wall faced a field with scattered rocks, no doubt hauled there from flower beds and manicured lawns and dumped where they would be out of the way.

Benny tugged the ivy away from the wall. Grabbing a white stone, he drew a crude bull's eye on the brick. The etching was faint, but it was enough. "Just get one in the circle, boy-o," Benny teased, but the twinkle in his eye made Tom smile. His friends gathered behind him, though Benny stood where he could easily judge Tom's accuracy.

Tom exhaled and tried to clear his mind. He couldn't concentrate properly. His thoughts were still going too fast. It all seemed so obvious now, the possibilities of what his Blood Magick could do. The potential. He was staring at a bunch of rocks like he expected one of them to introduce itself. Where he had momentarily felt powerful, back when the Master was coming after him, now he just felt silly.

"Well?" Zaina prompted.

"So far, it's anticlimactic," Benny murmured half under his breath. Tom scowled and concentrated harder. The rock under his gaze refused to lift and hurl itself at the shed.

"Do you need blood?" Mandy asked, clearly trying to be helpful.

"I want to see what I can do without cutting myself," Tom growled. So far, the results had been less than extraordinary. "Without blood. I should be able to…"

"It's like being on stage," Zaina said as though she were diagnosing him. "Performance anxiety. Sometimes people can't even speak, they become so intimidated in front of an audience."

"Would it help if we turned around?" Mandy asked. "We won't look."

"I will," Benny said quickly.

Zaina shrugged. "Me too."

"Right. If it helps him…" Mandy waved her arms and pivoted on her heel until her back was to him. The others shuffled around, not quite as dramatically.

With a wary glance at the group, Tom reached down, grabbed a rock, and threw it. It bounced off the wall. "Missed," cried Benny. Tom shot him a look under lowered brows. So much for not watching.

"Do you have a knife or a pin?" Zaina asked. "You're wearing your ring, aren't you?"

"Fine." Tom reached into his pocket to retrieve the tiny device he'd started carrying around with him. He'd bought a lancet in London. Diabetics used the small device to check blood sugars. It would produce a single drop and was a lot easier to control than the blade in the ring, which tended to cut much deeper than he needed. And though Lola could be annoying, she was right. This was a lot more sanitary.

The memory of the blood spear caused him to shudder inwardly. Yes. Control. It was all about the control. Though he'd told his friends about the attack, he hadn't mentioned anything about the spear or the dead Warlock.

He popped the device, and a sharp sting kissed his fingertip. A drop of blood obediently appeared. It was round and bright, and it looked like the drop that showed up yesterday in the Headmaster's office.

In the depths of the bubble, as though it were a crystal ball, Tom saw the Headmaster, heard him all over again, the news of his canceled trip, the trip everyone else was still going on. His isolation still gnawed at him. Worst of all, Tom still felt like he had been played for a fool.

I did fight him. He pulled that around him like armor. *Armor.* It cut his arm because Tom had ducked. It cut his arm because Tom was a better opponent for The Master than anyone gave him credit for. He had killed the Warlock. *He* was the one that defended their home. *He* was the one who stayed and defied The Master himself.

If it was so important to run and hide, then why hadn't there been reinforcements? Why had no one else stood up to that maniac? Why was it up to Tom when he had no assistance, no training, nothing to show for all he'd been through? Playing him for a fool? Well, it seemed as if *everyone* was playing him for a fool. Certainly, the Headmaster had his hand in that, as well as Thunderbolt. How great of a fool was he?

Tom felt the blood pounding in his ears, his teeth grinding against each other. His breath came slow and even. The sort of cold rage that burns so deeply that each breath stoked the flames until the white-hot burn tore at his core.

"It's not fair." He didn't know if he spoke it out loud and just then, he didn't care. He twisted the signet ring, watching the blood bubble and trickle across his fingers. All he had to do was to open the ring, to cut deeper, produce more blood...

"TOM!" Zaina's shout made him jump. A rock the size of his fist exploded from the ground under him and shot toward the wall. It slammed into the brick hard enough to shatter the old wall, tearing a hole wide enough for Tom to crawl through. It continued through the heart of the building. He could hear the crash and crunch of metal and plastic, and then the sickening blast as the rock shot through the other side.

Tom stared at the hole. He could see all the way through. The buildings which made up the school were thankfully far enough away to remain undamaged. He hoped. He wasn't altogether sure how far the rock had flown or even whether it was still in motion somewhere, tearing through whatever lay in its path.

Benny whistled. "Bull's eye."

CHAPTER
TEN

THE FOLLOWING MONDAY, Devlin found Tom the moment he sat down with his breakfast. He dropped into a chair across from Tom as though nothing had happened.

Well, not quite as though nothing had happened. He seemed more than a little subdued, but he was at least there and talking to him again. After walking away, and Lola calling Tom an idiot, Tom was afraid that the friendship might be over. It was a relief to have him back again, even if Devlin seemed more distant right now.

It's always awkward after a fight. Give it time.

"Hey." Tom nodded a hello. "Have you seen Lola?"

Devlin nodded. "She is coming." He hesitated, staring at his own plate as though he'd never seen eggs before. He tapped the rim with the tines of his fork while he worked out what to say. "You owe her an apology. You know that, yes?"

Tom stared. "For what? What did I do?"

Devlin dropped his fork and shoved the plate back away from him. "You...you are constantly talking about that girl, Zaina, and your new friends. About *your*...problems."

"What? I'm not allowed to talk about someone trying to kill me?"

"Do not get your back up." Devlin glanced over his shoulder. Satisfied they were far enough away from prying eyes, he added, "but she needs some time and attention too. She…cares about you. But you have to meet her halfway."

"What can I do? I mean…I'm pretty much a prisoner here. I can't even go on the stupid class trip for Global Studies. What am I supposed to do?"

"Just…" Devlin stopped and forced a smile on his face. He waved to someone over Tom's shoulder. Tom turned in time to see Lola walk up to the table. To his relief, her bright smile wasn't forced, and Tom couldn't help but smile back. That was the power Lola had. If she smiled, anyone around her smiled too. It was inevitable. If her smile disappeared, the day would become hollow and long, as though something was missing that couldn't be explained.

"Hi." She took a seat next to Tom and across from Devlin. "I heard they have the wards set at Harding. I guess you went back over the weekend to learn how to control your…gifts?"

It was, in part, reassurance that things were okay between them. But also, an admission that they were not. That she hadn't known for sure where he'd gone, whether he'd been in London or Harding felt strange. Even surreal. Normally, they would talk constantly. They hardly said a word to one another now.

Devlin shot Tom an unreadable look. It was evident what he meant, however. It was a continuation of the earlier conversation, but Lola was talking to Tom about *him*, and to change the topic over to her would look like he was avoiding the question.

"I was. I mean I've been there already." The image of the small brick shed being holed by the rock he threw still haunted him. It shouldn't have held together. The rock should have smashed, pulverized on the brick. Even if it did somehow manage to destroy the wall, it couldn't hold its shape long enough and hard enough to go through a riding lawnmower, a worktable, and the far wall. Mandy had run to the other side and retrieved the shot, still in the original shape. Thankfully it hadn't gone more than twenty meters past the building on the other side. He'd had nightmares about that rock crashing through one of Harding's walls into a classroom. Or worse, a student.

It was troubling that there was no impetus to hold or choose the rock altogether. In fact, the choice of missile was completely subconscious. True, he'd been trying to lob a stone earlier. But at the time of the actual rock launch, he had gotten lost in thought. A condition that had been occurring with alarming frequency lately.

Zaina explained after that she had called him several times, but Tom had ignored her, staring at something in his hand. He'd been tracing the drop of blood, playing with it over his finger. It was the Blood Magick then. So, did he *need* to bleed in order to do Magick? Could he do nothing without it? That couldn't be true, could it?

He could have blown up the Headmaster's office. He knew that as sure as he knew how to walk. He'd seen the room in basic geometrical shapes, the way things looked *after* they were destroyed and he knew, he *knew* how everything wanted to fly apart, how everything wanted to be destroyed, and how to allow it to happen. To break the tenuous bonds that held everything together.

That knowledge came from looking at his blood. It also came when he was angry, raging. It would have been better to rely on blood than to rely on an uncertain temper. If the Magick only worked when he was angry, it wasn't very helpful. *Wild Magick.* Uncontrollable power. Dangerous and unpredictable.

There had to be a way to control it. There had to. And as far as Tom could see, Harding was the best place to find the answers. It strengthened his resolve.

"I'm...I'm planning to ask to go there full time." He spoke the words in a rush. Lola's smile evaporated from her face as though it had never been. Tom added quickly to Devlin's frown. "I...I just think that I could get better instruction there. I mean for the...Blood Magick. A couple of classes every Saturday aren't going to cut it."

"I see," Lola said to the tabletop. "Do they have a Global Studies concentration there too, or..."

"It's a little different than here; I'd be taking a lot of magic-related courses. Kind of like you and Devlin with your Time Walking and Portal Jumping classes..." Tom let the sentence hang, hoping Lola would see the parallel between their situations.

"But you'd still be getting a university degree, right?" she asked, intent on getting her answer.

"Yes, of course, but I won't have as many Global Studies classes," he admitted.

"Your major..." Lola turned back to him, concern evident in her eyes.

"It doesn't really matter." Tom traced an old stain on the table with a finger. "I can't be in it anyway."

"Why not?" Devlin put off looking as though he were eating a lemon and became genuinely interested.

"I can't go on the stupid trip." Tom felt the fresh irritation from that disappointment.

"Why not?" Devlin sounded as though he were affronted as if this was all happening to him, not Tom.

"Because it's not safe," Lola answered for Tom. "One Professor couldn't protect him alone."

"I don't need protection," Tom grumbled before he could stop himself. "I mean..." his lip curled into a smile, "I could always throw a rock at him if I need to."

"No," Devlin shook his head, "I was not thinking. Lola is right. It is not safe. I am sorry, I know you'd been looking forward to this for a long time, but being out in the world when a powerful and questionably sane wizard like The Master is hunting you? No." He seemed to crawl into himself as if the very thought terrified him.

"I can't run and hide for the rest of my life."

"Of course not. No one is saying that." Lola placed her hand on Tom's arm. It was warm and comforting. For some reason, he wanted to shake it off, but he stayed still. He would have done almost anything to have her touch him like that and now that she was, he wanted to reject it. He tugged at the signet ring and twisted it to help him focus. "No one is saying for life, Tom, just for...now. Just for a little while until things are..."

Tom shook his head. "What? Different? Better? Nothing is going to change unless someone changes it, and I don't see anyone else..."

"You might not see it, but that does not mean it's not happening," Devlin shot back. "Headmaster Lianon is..."

"Afraid." Tom sat back, letting go of the ring. It also served as a way of brushing Lola's hand away. "He's afraid. He told me so himself."

"That means he's sane!" Lola protested.

"For all his talk about Elvin magic being stronger than human magic? If that were true, why should he be afraid of a mere human like The Master?"

"Are you sure his *is* human?" Devlin asked.

Tom clapped his mouth shut. He'd only seen the bottom of the man's face, and even that was in shadow. The Master might not be human? This was something he hadn't even considered before. Elf? Could he be an evil Elf? Well, no, he hadn't the height. But there were other kinds of creatures. That would certainly explain a lot. Maybe the Headmaster was in league with him? Some alliance between non-human types?

The thought seemed unworthy. On the other hand, maybe he just wanted to cover it all up, not have to deal with the embarrassment of a magical creature gone bad.

"I hadn't thought of that," Tom whispered. Devlin graced Lola with a pleased look as though he'd solved an unsolvable puzzle. "Does that mean I can trust the Headmaster?"

Lola did a double-take. "What? Where did that come from?"

"Well," Tom found his thumb was now on the ring, pressing against it. "Think about it. Suppose The Master isn't human. But he's all-powerful, right?"

"So?"

"So...maybe that's why Lianon isn't doing anything about this. Maybe he just doesn't want to go against a non-human."

"Tom, that's ridiculous," Lola scoffed. Devlin looked as though Tom had suggested that fish would make good furniture.

"No, hear me out. I mean, what if, just hypothetical, but what if it wasn't *just* The Master who is upset about this? What if it was all magical beings? I mean if humans," he gestured to himself as an example, "have Blood Magick, then High Elves would no longer be at the top of the magical food chain." He leaned forward, getting involved in his own theory, ignoring the saner part of himself telling him he was going absolutely crackers about now. "Would that upset the balance? I mean we're human. We're used to being told over and over again how High Elves are our betters in all things magical. What about other races? What happens if there's a Blood Mage? What if there was more than one? If I have a kid someday? Would he be a threat too? Maybe no one really wants humans to have magic at all."

"TOM!" Lola snapped. "Listen to yourself. You're talking paranoid nonsense. Worse, you're sounding kind of racist."

Tom gave her a blank stare. "Racist?"

"Well," Devlin temporized, "Speciesist." He had some trouble wrapping his mouth around the unfamiliar word. "But after all of this, you know that you can't link all magical beings any more than you can link all humans. I daresay you've met more than a few humans who were... well, evil. That applies to any of the other magical races."

An image of Jameson flashed in front of Tom's mind. "Yeah." Tom tried to force a laugh. "I mean, I was just throwing it out there for fun. You know, 'what if', like I said."

Lola was clearly unconvinced. "That's not something that would have ever occurred to you before, Tom. What's going on with you?"

"Nothing." Tom barked and held up a hand, to stop her, to steady himself...neither worked. He felt odd. Dizzy. "I'm sorry. You're right, I am on edge. I really am sorry. It's all this hiding and running. And every night I have to go home and hear my mother complaining about having to stay in some luxury flat or another and how terrible it is to have to stay home all day watching television and eating...well, I don't know what she's eating, but she's got nothing to complain about."

"Are you and your family having...problems?" Lola asked softly.

"No." Tom shook his head. "No, it's just a little stir crazy. I think we're just getting on each other's nerves." He waved it off. "Honestly, what really bothers me is that I understand why she's frustrated. I am too, but when she's upset, I know it's my fault and I feel...guilty, I guess."

"It's not your fault." Devlin objected.

"You did nothing to deserve this." Lola added, "you didn't ask to be stalked by a crazed Wizard."

"'Crazed'?" Devlin raised an eyebrow. "How do you know he's crazy?"

"Because he's stalking a child," Lola said in a very quelling tone. Devlin looked as though he wanted to argue the point, but he subsided. He probably argued it anyway. Telepathically. One more conversation Tom wasn't privy to.

"Anyway," Tom said as contritely as he was able, "I *am* sorry. I know I've been...not myself lately. And for that matter, you might have been right about me being an idiot." He saw the look of confusion on her face, though Devlin was deliberately staring at some distant image. "Last time we met, you called me an idiot," he explained.

Lola blushed. It was actually cute. "I shouldn't have called you an idiot."

"Yes, you should have. I was. I *am*. I just can't sit passively and wait for others to fight my battles for me. I know..." he cut off her rejoinder, "I know, I'm not ready to face him. I might not be ready for a very long time, I get that. But I have to start. I have to do *something* to..."

"...to keep moving?" Devlin asked. Tom thought about that for a moment, certain there was a trap somewhere in there, but unable to see it.

"I suppose so." Tom forced a smile. "At least I would feel like I'm trying. It's the passivity that's killing me."

"So, what are you going to do?" Lola asked hesitantly. Almost fearfully.

Tom took a deep breath. "I'm transferring. I'm going to learn how to use what I've been given."

"So...what does this mean...for us?"

Tom shot a glance at Devlin, as if you say, 'You wanted us to talk. Then leave already so I can do it!'

"If you will excuse me." Devlin stood and gathered his things. "I have to get ready for a quiz in Latin." He gave Tom another of those ambiguous looks that was probably meant to be significant and nodded once to Lola. He wandered off in the direction of the Library, but Tom saw him stop under the shade of the building, far enough to be out of earshot, but close enough to see.

It occurred to him that Devlin was watching in case he was needed. Not that he needed to. Lola could call him with her mind in an instant. He just wanted to stay close so he could get there faster if need be. The question was, did Devlin think Tom was going to need him? Or Lola? His words about paying attention to her echoed in Tom's ears. What had he really been saying? Had one of their 'private' conversations been about her reconsidering being Tom's girlfriend? Was Devlin trying to warn him, so Tom could be let down easy?

If that was the case, shouldn't he be trying that much harder to make sure that didn't happen?

He shook his head, trying to focus on what he needed to say here, now, to fix things between them. "Can we..." Tom swallowed and tried again. "Can we meet after dinner?"

"Just the two of us?" she asked, frowning a little.

"Yeah." Tom shrugged. "But not to talk about all of this. Just to be together. I feel like we haven't been alone in a while."

When they had first started dating, they had agreed to take things slow. They had met during the Summer program, Lola's first experience at The Academy. She'd been busy trying to catch up and coming to terms with a brother she didn't know she had, new magical abilities, and loads of family drama.

It wasn't until the Fall semester started that they got to spend any time together. Mostly, they'd spent their time cramming a full year of high school into a single semester. So, they snatched moments here and there during the week. On weekends, Lola and Devlin went home to be with their aunt, while Tom stayed behind.

Tom thought he'd finally get his chance over the Winter break, but Lola had to deal with her aunt's wedding, and he had to play chauffeur for his mom. When the Winter term rolled around, he had planned on slowly taking their relationship to the next level, whatever that might be, but that was cut short when the whole Blood Magick thing blew up.

He moved closer and took Lola's hands. The familiar spark was still there. He saw her relax and she smiled.

"When I change schools, I'll be allowed to come and go as I want on the weekends. We could go out on a proper date. But for now, I'd settle for a moonlight stroll with my best girl," he said, a shy smile on his face as he kissed her cheek.

"I can never say no to a stroll," she said, placing a light kiss on his lips. "As for the date, aren't you supposed to be in hiding?" she asked.

"I could come to your house, or you come to the London flat. We could get takeout, watch a movie. Nothing fancy, for now," he said, a hopeful expression on his face.

Lola spurted a laugh. "That actually sounds great, Tom. And by staying home, we'll have the added security of having parents close at hand, just in case."

Tom gave her a megawatt smile. He wasn't thrilled at having an audience, but they had to start somewhere. Lola's estate was huge, and he was sure they could find a safe spot to be alone. Besides, it was a lot warmer in Virginia at this time of year than it was in the UK.

He pulled her in for a tight hug and she wrapped her arms around him. They held each other for a while, and he rested his chin on the top of her head. He breathed her in, catching a faint scent of pears and vanilla. Lola always smelled so good.

"I would never let anything happen to you. You know that right?" he said.

She loosened her grip and looked up at him. "I'd never let anything bad happen to you either," she said. She had that fierce look in her eyes. The one she got when one of her family members was in danger or if someone was being rude to her friends. "I know you feel like this is all on you, but we're in this with you. Me, Devlin, and the others. We're here for you."

The emptiness Tom had been feeling shifted. Their other friends were Travelers and had no magical abilities. Lola and Devlin's magic was defensive at best. It was clear to Tom that he would face The Master alone. But after the last couple of days, it felt good to have someone in his corner.

"Thanks,' he replied simply. Lola rose on tiptoes and kissed his forehead. "You bet."

They heard the bell chime and started back toward the school, holding hands.

Tom felt himself relax, the knot in the pit of his stomach finally easing. Maybe he didn't have to give up everything. The world wasn't an either/or place. Absently, he spun his signet. Maybe it wasn't going to be such a bad day after all.

CHAPTER

ELEVEN

THE NEXT DAY, the Headmaster called Tom to his office just before lunch.

"I've spoken to your mother, Tom. Though she was worried about your safety, she agreed it was time for you to transfer to Harding Academy. It would have been a cleaner break for you to start right after Spring break, but we're only a few days into the new term and there's no time like the present." The High Elf waved to the Portal window behind him.

"Now? You want me to transfer now?" asked Tom. He should have been ecstatic. It's what he'd been hoping for. But just then, it felt like he was being rejected. Nervously, he spun the signet ring on his thumb.

"No, no. Nothing like that. Your mother will meet you at one-thirty in Miss Clementime's office to sign the paperwork. You'll start on Monday."

"But what about my friends?"

"You can tell them at lunch, though I doubt it'll come as much of a surprise. I'm sure you'll find a way to stay in touch. And besides, you'll be finishing out the week."

Tom nodded absently as he rose from the chair. "I can send you via

Portal, or we can meet in the Main Hall after lunch," Lianon said as he walked Tom to the door.

"I'd prefer to arrive by Door, if you don't mind," replied Tom. Arriving by Door already called attention to him. He didn't want to be seen arriving by Portal with the Headmaster, how lame would that be?

Once he'd said his goodbyes, and kissed Lola like a soldier going off to war, Tom went to his room to change into his street clothes.

The Headmaster was waiting for him in the Hall when he came down at one. As all the students were in class, they were alone.

"Come back to my office when you return. We have more to discuss," said the Headmaster as Tom opened a Door to Harding Academy.

IT WAS STILL lunchtime when Tom arrived at Harding Academy, and he made his way toward the cafeteria. On the way, he heard Benny call out to him.

"Hey Benny."

"Tom!" Benny caught up with Tom and they walked together for a while. "They're patching up the gardener shed."

Tom skidded to a halt. "Do they know?"

"That you fired a magical cannon point-blank at the side of the building?" Benny grinned. "Naw. Found out though, that the…uh… integrity of the building was compromised."

"What does that mean?"

"It means that the little-rock-that-could nearly took the entire building down. Apparently, the damage was worse than we thought. It weakened the walls, and the entire thing was close to falling." He grinned as though that were a great joke, then sobered. "Also, just so you know. I heard that the gardener sometimes goes out to the shed to sneak a smoke. If he'd been in there when it happened…"

"Yeah, but…" Tom felt a wave of fear, imagining that rock going through an innocent person because he hadn't thought to check to be sure the shed was empty. "If there was someone in there, he would have heard me throwing that first rock, heard us talking. He would have said something."

Tom needed to believe this. A sick feeling settled in the pit of his stomach.

"I suppose." Benny shrugged. "The point is, there was no one in there, and the next time we have you tear apart a building we'll check it out a bit more thoroughly. Besides, who knew you could even do..."

"TOM!" Zaina came running up to the two of them. "What are you doing here in the middle of the day on a Wednesday?"

"Yeah." Benny looked up and frowned. "That's actually a good question. Are you ditching class?"

"No..." Tom filled his lungs with clean air. Harding air. "No, I'm transferring."

"Here?" Zaina squealed. "Really? Oh, that's so cool! I have Mandy in my next class, I know she'll be thrilled too. Oh Tom, that's wonderful!" Zaina was one to usually keep her cool.

Her enthusiasm was infectious, and Tom found himself smiling. Where he'd felt lost, scared, and hopeless one moment, he now felt great. Looking back at some of his outbursts, it felt unreal, like he was thinking of someone else, someone who was...well, not Tom. He was glad he'd made peace with everyone at The Academy, including the Headmaster, before he left. They all agreed he'd been under a lot of stress and that it was normal for him to feel frustrated.

"I'm glad you're happy." Tom grinned. He hadn't noticed Zaina's eyes before, not really. Lola's blue eyes changed colors with her mood but rarely got all that stormy. Zaina's eyes were nearly black, with intense green flecks. She had a habit of staring intently at people, which was unnerving.

The girls were like night and day: where Lola was cautious, Zaina was impetuous. Lola was kind and earnest whereas Zaina was wild, gritty, and often sharp-tongued. Lola moved with a silent grace, almost regal. Zaina stalked; impervious to those around her, intent on her destination.

A guy could do a lot worse than having a friend like Zaina.

And here she was grinning from ear to ear because Tom was transferring to her school. It made Tom feel wonderful and proud, as though he was on the brink of discovering something entirely new.

Benny must have picked up on something because he laughed.

"What's so funny?" Zaina demanded.

"Nothing." Benny stopped and thrust his hand out to Tom. "Welcome to Harding," he said as Tom took his hand and shook it.

"Thank you." Tom grinned.

"Just...leave one or two buildings standing, will you?" Benny clouted him on the shoulder. Tom thought he might be blushing. His cheeks were warm, and he couldn't stop grinning.

"Did you tell him?" Zaina asked. "About the building almost coming down?"

"I told him."

"Can you imagine?" Zaina said with a certain amount of awe mixed with mischief. "You almost took down a hundred-year-old brick building with a rock."

"And the rock is unharmed, by the way," Benny added sardonically.

Tom looked for a response but came up empty. Zaina broke the silence, confirming Tom's fear.

"Is he *blushing*?" she teased, sharing an amused look with Benny.

"The most powerful Blood Mage in the world is blushing?" Benny was by far, enjoying this too much.

"I'm the *only* Blood Mage in the world." Tom reminded him.

"...and you are *definitely* blushing," Benny teased. "I never knew demolition could be embarrassing."

"All right, all right." Tom laughed. It was good to talk about silly things again, good to be among friends who didn't insist on telling him what to do or how to live. "Anyway, I have to meet my Mom at Miss Clementine's at one-thirty to do some paperwork and get my schedule."

"What are you going to major in?" Zaina looked over her shoulder as if expecting someone. It occurred to Tom that they were both going to be late for class so they could talk to him.

"Structural engineering, of course." Benny laughed and grabbed

Tom's upper arm. "Seriously, I'm glad you're coming here. I gotta go. Professor Greene gets cranky if you're late."

"Oh, I remember!" Zaina commiserated. "You better run."

Benny started to jog sideways, "When do you start?" he called over his shoulder.

"Monday!" Tom waved, but Benny was already off and running.

"Don't you have class too?" Tom was suddenly concerned for Zaina. He didn't want to get her into trouble before he even started.

"I do…" Zaina bounced on her heels and licked her lips. She looked as though she wanted to say something, but the time was running out on her. She reached up and kissed Tom's cheek. "Welcome to Harding." And with that, she was gone, fleeing across campus as though she were running the fifty-yard dash.

Tom stood in pleasant shock. One hand over the spot her lips had caressed his cheek. He wasn't sure how he felt about being kissed by someone other than Lola. On one hand, it was kind of nice. On the other…he still had a date with Lola on Saturday night.

It's a friendly welcome. She's just happy I'm here, he told himself firmly.

Soon he was alone in the quad, all the students having found their classes. He found himself grinning like a fool. "It's a good day," he said to the air. Harding air.

It really had been a rather *nice* welcome.

He walked back to the admin building, slowly twisting the signet ring.

CHAPTER

TWELVE

THERE WAS a cozy fire crackling to itself in the corner of Lianon's office. A footman entered the room from the back while Tom stood bemused. He placed a tea set on the table between two wingback chairs.

Not for the first time, he thought how the room almost looked like something from a gentlemen's lounge in the 1800s, like something out of one of those period pieces on the BBC that his sister liked to watch. Tom fidgeted in the school uniform. Shouldn't he be in tails and idly swirling a drink in an oversized glass? Holding a cigar? Perhaps folding a newspaper? Of course, no one read newspapers anymore. He allowed himself a moment to chuckle over trying to fold an iPad instead.

"Tom!" Headmaster Lianon breezed in, his robes billowing as he walked. He smiled, seeming to be genuinely pleased to see Tom.

"Please. Sit." He swept a hand toward the chairs and waited for Tom to sit before choosing the other. Of course, this was a mere formality. They had played out this scenario often enough for Tom to know which chair the Professor preferred.

Lianon sighed as though taking weight off his feet was a relief. Regardless of species, everyone sighed when tired or deeply comfortable. It underscored that the Headmaster was old, something Tom had already known, but hadn't thought about before. No wonder he was so cautious. Caution was something that came with age, after all.

Lianon turned to the tea set and lifted the pot. "Shall I pour?"

"Uh...sure." Tom was a bit confused. Suddenly he was being treated as if nothing had changed? As if this were any other high tea with the Headmaster? He tried to figure out what's changed, what was happening. He accepted the teacup and saucer graciously, but his guard was up. It was like waiting for the other shoe to drop.

Lianon took a sip and smiled. "Ah. Peach Cobbler!" The man really liked his flavored teas. Tom took a sipped and made the expected enjoyment sounds. The tea *was* good. He leaned back in the chair.

"Well," he took a deep breath and continued with the air of a man who needed to say something he didn't want to. "All the paperwork is complete. You're on your way to Harding."

"Thank you, Sir." Tom wasn't sure exactly what he was thanking him for, but it seemed appropriate. "Thank you for approving my transfer."

"I could see how heavily this weighed on you. I had to work out details with Harding, they needed to upgrade their security, but everything is all set." Tom picked up the cup again. "I daresay, you will be missed," the Headmaster said, taking a sip of tea.

Then you should have trained me. Tom cleared his throat. Where had that thought come from? He'd spent two entire days feeling like his old self and suddenly now? When the Headmaster was making such an effort? "Thank you, Sir" was all Tom could vocalize.

Lianon studied him from the bottom of his gaze for a moment and only grunted. Tom wondered if the Headmaster could read his mind. He'd started to get used to the idea that his thoughts were closed off from the High Elf. Maybe Tom had something in his voice that made him sound ungrateful?

Or were his thoughts clear again, to the Headmaster? Tom wasn't sure how he felt about that.

"Honestly, Sir. I am grateful for all your efforts. I really am. The restrictions have made me irritable and...unpleasant on occasion, and I am sorry for that." *Though running and hiding wasn't exactly* my *decision, was it?* "But I think that Harding will be helpful."

Lianon nodded but said nothing. He straightened in his chair and studied the fire while sipping tea. "Though you will have personalized instruction, you must remember that Blood Magick has not been seen in a long time. There is no one who can tell you in detail how to control this power or what exactly it can do. You and your instructors will be learning together, I'm afraid."

Tom wasn't hungry, but he wished there were snacks on the tray. It would have made the conversation less awkward. "I know. But I have it, and...I need to learn how to use it."

"How *not* to use it." Lianon corrected him. "Don't misunderstand me," he spoke over Tom's initial reaction, "learning control over power like yours is of primary importance. But part of control is *not* using your power until you *choose* to and not allowing the power to decide when and where it will be used. Power...all power, is mindless and erratic. Learning the art of *not* using it gives you control."

Tom struggled to work this through in his mind. "So, I'm supposed to pretend I don't have Blood Magick?"

"Oh, no. Quite the opposite. Think of it as an emotion. If you suppress your feelings, bottle them up, you're likely to fly into rage over something trivial. In fact, all the suppressed anger comes out all at once, so you might scream over something as simple as a frustrating phone call. In your case, however, the "scream" could have very severe ramifications."

Tom tore his gaze away from the fire and looked at Lianon. "Sir, I'm not sure I fully understand what you're saying. It sounds as though you're trying to tell me something without actually saying it."

"No." Lianon set his cup next to Tom's. "At least, not that I know of. Sometimes, as people age, they find that their words are taken as great wisdom when all they really are talking about is the weather. What I *am* saying is that if you are beginning to learn, beginning to...experiment...then this should be your first step in learning to master the power."

Tom felt heat rising on his cheeks. Lianon had already caught him experimenting once before. He seemed to know, or guess, that Tom had kept on trying. Did he know about the garden shed? No. That wasn't possible. If Lianon knew that Tom had passed a rock through a brick building, this meeting wouldn't be as cordial as it was right now. He'd be getting lectured about acting impetuously or something. And likely, he'd have told Miss Clementine and the matter would have been discussed with his mother earlier that day.

"I will...keep that in mind, Sir. But may I ask, how will *not* using power help if I should be attacked again?"

Lianon chuckled under his breath. "Tom, there is more to you than the Blood Magick, and more to a fight than brute force. Winning a fight isn't always about overpowering your opponent. You just need make use of *all* the skills you have."

"I'm pretty good at tennis," Tom said flatly. "Are you saying I should challenge The Master to a game?"

Lianon grinned. "That I would like to see. Those robes flapping in every direction as he tries to get the ball. No, Tom and don't be deliberately argumentative. What I mean is that first and foremost, you are a Traveler. You've completed all levels of our Magic and Incantation classes. Yet, by your own admission, you neither used your Key to flee, nor to fight when you were faced with the Master."

Tom opened his mouth to speak, but nothing came out. The Headmaster reached into a pocket and produced a small manual that Tom recognized instantly. It was the Traveler's Handbook. He held out the book and Tom took it.

How long had it been since he'd paged through it? He and his friends followed the rules and used a handful of useful spells like the one to call a flame or a drink of water. Or to make a window in your Door to ensure the coast was clear before opening it. But the rest? Not so much.

Tom opened the Handbook to a random page. It was the incantation to make yourself invisible for 15 seconds. *That* would have been useful, if he would have remembered it.

Lianon was observing him with an unreadable expression.

"So, you're saying that before learning new things, I should be mastering what I've already learned?"

"Yes. Like most Travelers, you've taken your Key for granted. You use it as a quick way to get from point A to point B. But there is so much more to Traveling and I thought it was high time you were reminded. Especially since you chose Global Studies as a major."

Tom was dumbfounded. The Headmaster was absolutely right. When Tom chose Global Studies, he wanted to improve the Traveling Network, and make people accountable. He'd forgotten to hold himself accountable.

"You're right, Sir," he said. "I've been ranting that no one will teach me when I already know a lot; or did."

He waved the Handbook. "I'll memorize all the incantations."

Lainon laughed. "I forget how literal you can be. Yes, Tom. Refresh your memory. And when you get to Harding, learn the skills they have to teach you. All of it will come in handy. But most of all, keep working on mastering your emotions. That way, you'll have access to all your skills in a crisis and your go-to won't be Blood Magick. That particular skill should be used sparingly, and never in the heat of anger."

Tom dropped his chin to his chest. While the Headmaster had a valid point, Tom felt chastised. He'd been scared and angry when he'd wrestled the Warlock. That's what Lianon was getting at. Tom looked down at the Handbook, realizing once more how any number of spells could have gotten him out of the scrape and prevented it altogether.

Tom didn't like the guilty feeling that crept up from the pit of his stomach. Anger would feel better, and he felt the subtle shift as he bristled and got to his feet. "Will that be all, Sir?" Tom asked curtly.

Lianon rose too, but he looked sad, almost defeated. Lianon held out his hand. "For now, at any rate, Tom. It will have to do for now."

Tom took his hand cautiously, though what he might have been expecting to happen, he couldn't have said. He shook the Headmaster's hand and a bittersweet regret blossomed in his heart. Despite everything, Lianon had been his Headmaster for some time and had been in Tom's corner, so to speak. He'd been a father figure, of sorts. Leaving him now, and with resentment, didn't feel right. He tried to think of something to say that might ease the moment, but he couldn't think of anything. In the end, he let his hand drop to his side and he walked out on the Headmaster and his office for possibly the last time.

He didn't look back.

THIRTEEN

"I GUESS…" Devlin didn't look quite at Tom. "I don't understand. Yes, I will miss you, but it is not like you are dying. You are just going to a different school. I'll see you when you come to our house to see Lola, and we'll be studying there ourselves during the Summer."

"Sure." Tom was still on edge from the 'exit interview' he'd had with the Headmaster. Now Devlin was acting weird and getting the reason out of him was like pulling teeth. "So…" he held his hands out as though he was expecting Devlin to give him something, at the very least some kind of hint as to why he didn't seem to think this was a good idea.

"It's just that…you're making permanent solutions for temporary problems."

"What do you mean?" Tom felt his skin prickle, the way it did when he was angry. He fought that down. *I can get angry without using my power. I already know how NOT to use it. Besides, this is what I wanted, right? An explanation. The fact that I don't agree with his reasoning doesn't mean I have to get all bent out of shape about it.*

"Well…" Devlin looked miserable. He also looked a little…nervous? "You are making life-altering changes. Your major, your school, your… friends. All because of The Master. You're safe here, your family is safe.

There's been no sign of him since that day. Yet, you're turning your whole life inside out. Regardless of the outcome, you're not the same, Tom."

"Well, being hunted by a supervillain will change a person." It was all Tom could do to keep from snapping the words. Even so, they came out sharper than intended.

"But that's the point. You're not being hunted *here*. Nor at home. And clearly, the adults don't think you'll be hunted at Harding Academy. Perhaps The Master has given up. Perhaps he's already been dealt with by the proper authorities. Either way, it's over. Then what? Will you come back to The Academy? Are you going to walk away from your new friends too?"

Tom sighed. So, this was what it was all about. He was *jealous*. Well, that put a different spin on things entirely. "I'm not walking away," he explained patiently, feeling a little superior now that he had Devlin figured out. "Like you said, we'll be seeing each other. A lot. I promise. I'm only going to a school where I can learn the most important thing I need to. I have to learn to control what I am. Who I am."

"And who is that?" Devlin looked at him with accusations in his eyes. "Who are you? Because I don't know anymore."

"I'm still me." Tom snapped, sick of the direction this conversation was going. "Everyone is playing games and tip-toeing around like I am some sort of time bomb ready to go off. But I'm still *just* me! I don't have the luxury of waiting around with my hands tied. Why does no one here understand that? Yeah, my family is safe – *for now*. You weren't there! You didn't see how The Master just popped each and every ward like a piece of gum. You didn't see the destruction, the casual way he threw his Warlocks into battle as if they meant nothing to him. He's not giving up, not in the long term, short term, or any other term."

Tom scrubbed at his face. "How is it that I can talk my damn head off and *still* no one listens to me? I've been saying this since the night of the fight, and let me assure you, that *was* a fight. It wasn't any test with number two pencils and there was no looking at your neighbor for the right answer." He ignored Devlin's blink of surprise. "I *fought*

The Master. I stood up to him and *I* got away. No one does that against that kind of opponent. No one. Yeah, I'm leaving for a different school. I'm not really changing my major, only delaying it. But I *refuse* to sit here like a coward and pray the big bad wolf goes away."

He stepped back, trying to calm himself, but it was too late. "For that matter, my major would have been delayed here too. Half the Middle Eastern Studies grade was built around the trip that *I can't go on because of HIM!*" Tom flailed his arms in frustration.

"They would let you make up the grade..."

"By reading out-of-date books? By *not* experiencing the *entire point of the class*? Yeah, that would be great, wouldn't it? Meanwhile, all my classmates are sitting around sharing memories of the experience. What am I going to contribute, huh? I can tell them about my Mom going stir-crazy in our flat. I can tell them how sick I am of eating take-away every weekend or of hearing Tabitha whine that she can't see her friends." He clenched his fist against the tide of anger that came out, but he was powerless to stop it.

"I know it's hard..."

"No. No you don't. How could you know that? Is there a powerful Sorcerer after you too? Do you feel guilty every time your mother or sister sighs? How can you know that?"

"I miss you," Devlin mumbled.

"I already told you *twice*. I'll be coming back!" His thumb found the signet ring.

Devlin's eyes were on his hand. "No. I mean." Devlin backed up a step. "I miss you now. I miss the guy you were before the fight. I really miss *him*."

Tom felt the anger drain out of him. What was it that Lianon had said about repressing emotion? He was still irritable, but Devlin's quiet reprimand took the wind from his sails. "Look, I'm sorry. I just get frustrated when I keep explaining the problem and no one..."

"...agrees with you?" Devlin finished.

"...listens." Tom said quietly. "Maybe that's something I need to work on too. Dev, I have to do this."

Devlin nodded. He wasn't happy, but he no longer objected. "I know."

Tom searched for some neutral ground, something besides saying he was sorry all the time. "I have a date with Lola on Saturday." He tried to look into his friend's eyes. Devlin lifted his gaze and shot him a look.

"I heard. Lola was…excited." He stared at Tom for a beat. "I don't want Lola hurt."

"We decided to stay at your place," he said, hoping to mollify Devlin.

"Tom." Devlin took a step back. Tom noticed that his fists were clenched. Was Devlin planning on hitting him? "Are you planning to break up with her? Because if you're tying her up into all these knots emotionally and then plan to lower the blow when she thinks you're planning this really special night…"

My God, he does want to fight me.

"Don't be stupid." Tom crossed his arms over his chest to show Devlin he wasn't going to fight him. "I would never hurt Lola like that. Besides, it was *your* idea!"

"I said 'pay attention to her', not lead her on or give her false expectations."

"It's not like that."

"Then what is it, Tom? I don't know you anymore."

"I LOVE HER!" Tom screamed. It was getting to be too much. Running, hiding, no one listening. Tom listened. He listened to Devlin, he tried to do the right thing, the thing Devlin told him to, and it blew up in his face. *Now do you finally understand, Dev? This is what I have to live with all the time.*

"So, we came back around to the first question. Who are you? Because you're not the Tom I know." Devlin seemed unconvinced.

"Are you going to forbid Lola to go out with me?"

"You know I can't." Devlin sounded as though he wished he could. "Besides, I already tried."

"Dev," Tom said reasonably, "We aren't even leaving the property. It's not like I'm taking her out where the Master can get her or something. This is a pointless argument. Not only will you be around to check up on us, but Lola can call you telepathically if she needs you. I'm not planning on doing anything that could hurt her. If anything, I'm trying to reassure her everything will be okay once I leave."

Except Zaina's kiss upon his cheek still lingered there. He had not forgotten that.

"I know Tom wouldn't." Devlin agreed. "But *you*? I just don't know."

"I'm STILL ME!" Tom no longer cared if he attracted attention. He'd answered the question several times already, hadn't he? "I. WILL. NOT. HURT. HER!" He put his face close enough to Devlin's that if Lola's brother wanted to hit him, he was easily within reach.

Devlin's fists were no longer clenched, but as he turned away there was doubt in his eyes and a resigned expression upon his face.

CHAPTER
FOURTEEN

WHEN HIS LESSONS with Professor Montague were done for the day, Tom went home to the London flat to grab a few things from his room and see his mom. They had agreed he should stay at Harding for the weekend, to get settled and to hang out with his new friends.

He hadn't mentioned that he was heading to Lola's instead of back to Harding, and she hadn't asked. She was busy making plans to see her London friends, finally. Apparently, though the Council of Earthly Magical Beings had not yet apprehended The Master, they had identified a few of his minions and were now in the process of infiltrating his ranks. They were hopeful this would yield information about The Master's plans and the whereabouts of his lair.

Meanwhile, Arabella had been assigned a magical bodyguard. So long as she took them along, she was now free to resume her daily activities. One had been assigned to Tabitha as well.

"Don't I get one?" asked Tom, only half-joking.

"You are under constant supervision at school. I should think the staff at Harding will keep you as safe as you were at The Academy," she replied, adding the final touches to her make-up.

"I'm happy for you and Tabitha," he replied and kissed his mother's cheek before heading out.

"Tom?" She turned and gave him a once over. "Why are you wearing a dress shirt and cologne?"

Blast! She'd been so engrossed with herself, Tom thought she hadn't noticed.

"We dress for dinner at Harding Academy," he lied smoothly.

"I'm assuming you'll be wearing the school tie?" she asked eyeing his jeans and sneakers. Tom looked down at himself and replied, "My dress pants, shoes, tie, and robes are at school."

She nodded and merely said, "Well, have fun. Call me on Wednesday for an update."

"Yes, Mam," Tom said and left the room.

THOUGH IT WAS five pm in the UK, it was lunchtime in Virginia. He felt a little silly to be dressed up for a lunch date, but desperate times called for desperate measures.

Once in the Evers' courtyard, he walked up to the front door and rang the doorbell.

When the door opened, the smile Tom was flashing wavered. It was Devlin.

"Don't you look smart," he said, stepping aside to let Tom in.

"Thank you. I wanted to look good for my date."

"Lola! Tom's here!" bellowed Devlin.

The person who came rushing out of the kitchen wasn't Lola. It was Phyllis, their aunt, cradling an infant in her arms.

"Goodness gracious, Devlin! You know better than to be hollering in the house," she crooned in her southern belle accent as she swatted at Devlin. "Go on and fetch your sister properly."

"Yes, Phyllis," he said with a half bow and turned on his heels. He kept an eye on Tom as he went up the winding staircase.

"Come in. Come in, Tom!" exclaimed Phyllis as she turned a cheek to receive his obligatory kiss. Phyllis was like Lola and Devlin's mother, and she was one of the nicest women Tom had ever met.

As she led him to the parlor, she introduced Tom to Lulu. He cooed over the baby and asked about her twin brother.

"Leo is with his father in the study," she replied and offered him something to drink. He asked for a ginger ale and settled on one of the couches.

"I'm sure Lola will be down in a moment," said Phyllis, checking on the sleeping child.

"They refuse to nap in their beds and keep us up all night when they don't get enough sleep. It's a paradox, I know. This way, we get a little peace and quiet before lunch. Speaking of which, cook has prepared a feast for you and Lola. I know you wanted to do something special, but I also know your hands are tied at the moment, so to speak."

"Thank you, that's very thoughtful. When this blows over, I'll take Lola out on a proper date. I promise," he said solemnly.

Phyllis threw her head back and laughed so loudly that the baby jerked but did not wake.

"Oh sugar, you don't need to impress me! And I'm sure you don't need to impress Lola. She'd take a picnic in the gazebo or a bowl of candy in the game room over a fancy dinner any day!"

Tom smiled. That did sound like his Lola. She was unassuming and didn't like to call attention to herself. Of course, she would shy away from going out where everyone would be looking at her.

As if on cue, Lola strode into the parlor. Tom shot up.

"Lola! You look beautiful!" he said, taking in the skirt and sweater she was wearing.

"You sure do, honey," piped in Phyllis. "But then again, you always do." She rose too, smiled at Lola and Tom, and headed toward the study.

THEY'D PICKED up the basket in the kitchen and settled on a blanket in the gazebo.

"I have a surprise," said Tom.

"Is it in your bag?" asked Lola, clapping her hands in excitement.

"I wanted to take you to Paris." Tom waited for Lola's coo of appreciation. "But..."

"But you can't Travel."

Tom nodded. "So, I brought a little of Paris to you." He dug into the bag and produced something with a dramatic flourish. "Bienvenue à Paris!" Tom held up a model of the Eiffel Tower. One of the legs was caught on a napkin, breaking the solemnity of the moment, but it made Lola laugh and that made it all worth it. He'd all but forgotten the joyous music of her laughter, and when he could be the one to bring it out, it made him feel somehow as though he'd made the world a better place, at least for a short time.

"It's smaller than I would have thought from all the pictures."

Tom turned the tower over and looked at it as if he'd never seen it before. "Trick photography." He grinned, "See?" He held the model over her head. "Looks a lot taller now, doesn't it?"

Lola was trying not to laugh. "Oh yeah, I see it now."

Tom set it down at the end of the blanket and reached into the bottom of his bag, "we need to toast the occasion!" He laughed at her expression. Tom pulled a bottle of French sparkling water and reached for the glasses the cook had included in the basket. He poured them each a glass.

"To our first real date!" he said clinking his glass to hers.

"It's not our first date!" scoffed Lola. "Is it? It can't be," she added, frowning now.

"Um, yeah, it is. We've never been anywhere alone together. I mean, we're not really alone now," he said, pointing at one of the upper windows.

Lola turned around and saw Devlin watching them, making no attempt to hide the fact. She scowled at him, and he stepped into the shadows.

"He's a little overprotective,' she said, taking a sip of her fizzy water.

Tom didn't reply to the comment as he didn't want to kill the mood.

"Shall we eat?"

They ate in silence for a time, content to be together in the shade of the gazebo. Finally alone. It was a lovely Spring day and, though the air had a bit of bite, it was better than the cold rain of the northern Scottish Coast where Harding was located.

Eventually, Lola set her plate down on the blanket and picked up the miniature. She turned it over and looked at it from different angles. "I've never been to the Eiffel Tower before but would like to see the real one someday...with you." She didn't look up from the model.

Tom stopped chewing in the middle of a mouthful. He tried to get to the end of that bite before speaking, feeling like a startled cow with a mouthful of fodder. "Me too." He managed to croak that out without making a pig of himself, but it was a very near thing. He took a sip of his water and cleared his throat. When he thought it was safe to talk again, he set his plate next to hers. "I know that sitting on a blanket in your backyard isn't really the most romantic setting for a date."

"I like it. It's fun."

Tom smiled at her, but of course, neither of them really had a choice, did they? "I probably should have let The Master keep my Key." He spoke to the trees behind them.

"Tom." Lola shuddered, "a Traveler without a Key?"

"Is it any worse than having a Key and not being able to use it?" Tom asked reasonably. "I have it. It's here and yet I have to bring a girl on a picnic to her own backyard and make the 'best of it'."

"I know it's frustrating..."

"No, you don't." Tom leaned over to her. It was comforting to smell her perfume. Something mixed with lilac. Vanilla? "You don't mind this because there's no choice. There's no choice because I can't go anywhere. I can't go anywhere because of *him*."

"Tom, please don't get upset. Don't ruin a good date because of The Master. He can't have this too."

Tom stared for a moment. First of all, he hadn't realized he'd been shouting. Secondly, it wasn't the Master he'd been referring to. It was Headmaster Lianon who had arranged for the travel restrictions. It was the Headmaster who had Tom hiding under rocks in London. But, on further reflection, The Master was also at fault, he'd give her that.

"It's a beautiful day, and the food is delicious." She looked down at the nearly empty plate, considering it for a moment. Then she gave a tiny shrug, probably meant for herself, and dug in again. She ate with relish, packing away more food than most girls Tom knew. He knew Lola wasn't into exercise, so he assumed all her worrying and planning kept her fit.

"Yeah," he looked up and took in the beautifully manicured grounds of the Evers Estate. He remembered Devlin's words of advice and tore himself from the track his mind had been on, despairing over what he couldn't change. He thought to try a different approach.

"I'd love to visit Paris with you. It would be fun."

"Don't you have a house there?"

"Yes," Tom played a moment with the remainder of the food, "But being there with my family...well, that's really not the same thing. I mean, alone with you would be...nicer."

"I think so too." Lola smiled. She set down her fork and reached for the model. "Is that where this came from?"

Tom laughed. "No. I went home to see Mam after class and grabbed it from my room in London. That and the sparkling water were the only 'French' things I could locate. I know, it's stupid."

"It's not stupid," Lola spun the toy. "I think it's sweet and clever." She lifted the model over Tom's head. "Now you have to look up and see how tall it is."

Tom obliged. For a moment, it really did look like the real thing, but that only made him miss Traveling even more. He hated not being able to go where he wanted to and when he wanted to go. It was like being grounded. No wonder his mom and sister were chomping at the bit to leave the house.

"Tom?" Lola interrupted his musing. Tom shook the bitterness that kept returning to him. It was like it rose of its own accord every once in a while, even after Tom was sure he'd worked through it.

He looked up and forced a smile on his face. He didn't want to spook her and ruin the date. It was going well.

There was pecan pie for dessert and a thermos of coffee. They kept the conversation light during dessert and Lola suggested going for a walk.

"Is that safe?" Tom asked with a hint of sarcasm. For the life of him, he couldn't fathom why he was being so snippy.

Thankfully, Lola missed the sarcasm and replied, "Of course. We'll stay on the grounds. We have a state-of-the-art security perimeter."

They followed the path around the estate, holding hands.

After a while, Lola broke the silence. "Tom, can I ask a question without you getting angry?"

She spoke softly and gave his hand a squeeze. It was meant to reassure him. But all it did was put his back up. He mumbled, "sure."

"Why didn't you summon a Door when The Master came into your house with his Warlocks?"

He gritted his teeth and willed himself to stay calm. Lola wasn't accusing him of anything. She just wanted to know. How could he explain it to her?

"He kidnapped my sister. He made manipulated some kids into attacking me as soon as I stepped out of The Academy. He was about to destroy my house. I had to stand up to him, once and for all."

"But what did you accomplish?"

"I won, didn't I?" he shot at her, insulted by her question.

"Do you really believe that? You and your family are in a self-imposed witness protection program..."

"Self-imposed? Are you kidding? We didn't choose this!" he shouted. He hadn't had the chance yet to let her know their exile was finally over, with bodyguards for his mom and sister, so they could move about.

Lola dropped his hand and took a step back.

"Maybe you should go," she said.

"Why?"

She gave him a stony glare.

"I've been looking forward to a day to just chill out. Can we just drop the subject? It was going so well. All I wanted was some time alone with my girlfriend. Is that too much to ask?"

He reached for her hand, but she pulled away from his grasp. When he moved closer to her, she put a hand up, manifesting a shield between them. She had never used magic against him.

This was the last straw.

"You don't trust me!"

"I trust you, Tom." Her quiet rejoinder made his outburst sound even more childish. "But I think you should go back to Harding now. It's getting late and there must be a curfew in effect."

"We haven't even watched a movie. It's barely seven in Scotland. Why?" Even to his ears, he sounded more whinny than angry.

Lola dropped the shield. "Since you triggered the...the Blood Magick, you've been...different. It's changed you."

"Of course it did," Tom said irritably. "I have these powers I can't control, and..."

"No. I mean...it's changed *you*, and not for the better, Tom." She started walking briskly down the path. "Let's go back to the gazebo."

He let her walk ahead of him. "Are you afraid of me?" he finally said.

She paused and seemed to consider her words before turning back to look at him. "I'm not afraid of you, Tom. I'm afraid *for* you."

The sad, resigned look in her eyes was too close to pity for Tom's liking. He fumed but said nothing. He followed her mutely along the path. When they got back to the Gazebo, someone had taken the remains of their picnic away. Only the Eiffel tower remained, propped up on one of the benches next to a scowling Devlin.

He stood when they approached, arms crossed like a club bouncer.

Lola placed a hand on his chest and pushed him gently. "I've got this."

She picked up the Eiffel Tower and handed it to Tom.

"Thanks for a lovely date. Good night, Tom."

Tom swiped the miniature and smashed it with his bare hands. He through the remains at Devlin's feet, pulled out his Key and left without a backward glance.

CHAPTER
FIFTEEN

WHEN TOM GOT BACK to Harding Academy, dinner was over. Students were heading to their respective common rooms or heading out. The school was in a rather remote part of the country and there wasn't much to do unless you were prepared to walk to the nearest town.

Though students were allowed to leave school grounds, they were encouraged to be discreet and not travel in large groups. First, to ensure that they didn't call attention to their school, which appeared to the rest of the world as just the ruins of a rundown Castle. But also, to maintain the peace for the few neighbors that the school did have.

Tom made his way to the common room he'd been assigned to and was happy that his new friends weren't around to witness his black mood. He was also relieved to see that he still hadn't been assigned a roommate.

He busied himself by putting away his clothes in the provided wardrobe. The repetitive task helped to clear his mind and he got through it quickly.

While he was placing his books and other knick-knacks in the small bookcase, a picture fell out from between some books. It was one of those instant sepia photographs, taken at his birthday party last August. Had it only been seven months since all hell had broken loose?

He and Lola were posing dramatically for the camera. For the 20s Speakeasy theme, everyone had been assigned a well-known character from the era. Lola was portraying Zelda Sayre, a novelist, painter, and socialite. Tom played her husband, F. Scott Fitzgerald, an American novelist and screenwriter.

They looked so happy, so carefree. Still holding the photograph, Tom sat on the bed and scrubbed his face with his other hand. He shouldn't have smashed the Eiffel Tower miniature, let alone thrown the pieces at Devlin's feet. He might as well have smashed their relationship.

He shook his head in bewilderment. He hadn't raised his voice. Or had he? He tried to pry the memory from his mind, but all he remembered was legitimately asking why she wanted him to leave. *She was afraid? For him?*

She had made it sound like she was afraid he was going nuts, and not because he was The Master's prey of choice. He would have understood if she'd been afraid for herself. Not that he would hurt her; she had to know he never would do that. But then again, she manifested an energy shield to keep him away. If anything, it would make sense that she would want to keep her distance so the Master wouldn't use her to get to him. That would make sense. He would understand *that*.

He suddenly felt cold and bone-weary. It was too early for bed, so he opted for a shower. He grabbed his shower caddy and towel and headed for the communal washrooms. The showers here weren't as nice as those at The Academy, but the steaming hot water felt really good. He lathered up quickly then leaned into the spray and stood still, allowing the heat to run over him. It did little to ease the thoughts that ran rampant through his mind, but the tenseness of his shoulders melted under the spray.

The water began to cool, and Tom came to, suddenly realizing that he had been standing there far too long. His time was up.

He dried himself roughly. The texture of the towel felt like sandpaper and that was what he wanted. It was what he needed.

Tom dressed in sweatpants and headed back to his dorm room. The common room was busier now, but Tom didn't see anyone he knew. Back in his room, his mind kept going over the incident with Lola. All he wanted was to spend a regular day with his girlfriend. He had hoped it would bring them closer, not further apart.

Had they broken up? Both Lola and Devlin had said that he has changed. At first, he thought they were ganging up on him. But then again, even Tom had to admit he was acting like a crazy person. He could feel the rage building inside him again, like water slamming against the wall of a dam.

They'd told him not to bottle up his emotions. But every time he tried to speak about them out loud, no one listened. Or they told him to relax and let the adults handle it. It was so frustrating. He debated sending Lola a note, but in his present state, it might make things worse. No, he needed to release the tension. He needed to spar.

One person came to mind: Arturo. He would make a great sparring partner. Tom hadn't seen his nemesis since the altercations with Jameson's goons. Truth be told, he couldn't think of Arturo as a nemesis anymore. The guy had stepped up to save his neck and, though he wouldn't call him a friend, they'd left things on friendly terms.

Bolstered by the thought, Tom left the safety of his room. He stopped a few people and asked if they knew Arturo. It seemed the guy was well known, but not well-liked. It took five tries to find someone who'd have a clue as to where Tom might find him.

"He likes to hang out in the gym," one girl said, elbowing her friend with a giggle.

"Why is that funny?" asked Tom.

"He trains without a shirt and waves to his adoring fans through the window of the observation deck," replied the other girl. She was giving Tom a thorough once over that was making him uncomfortable.

Before he'd met Lola, he'd never dated anyone. He knew he was handsome, but he'd never gotten such lascivious looks while at The Academy. Then again, most of his friends were straight guys. At his regular high school, he'd hung out with the D&D crowd. Though there had been girls in the group, everyone was focused on their roles and not each other's real personas.

He thanked the girls and left, feeling their gaze as he left the room.

WHEN HE GOT to the gym, he went to Coach Hanover's office. He figured he needed to ask permission to use the facilities. In light of the episode in the dungeon, he thought it best to have a teacher aware of his intentions. Coach Hanover wasn't there; he was probably at home with his family. Did Fairies have families? Children? Homes? Tom had never thought to ask. As far as he knew, Fairies might live in the garden out back.

A loud banging sound caught Tom's attention. It was coming from the gym. Through the window, Tom saw a guy with dark hair shooting hoops in one of the gym sections. He was clearly using magic because he hovered near the ring and slam dunked the ball. It has to be Arturo. He opened the door and walked in.

As he approached, he called out, "Hey, Arturo!"

The guy turned and cocked his head. It wasn't Arturo. He was holding the ball at chest level, like he was about to pass. Before Tom could even blink, the guy shot him the ball. It came at him with unnatural speed, given the distance between them. Instinct had Tom put his hands out to stop the ball; even if it had been thrown in a casual game of pickup, Tom would likely not have caught it. He wasn't all that athletic, and he'd gotten used to jocks throwing balls at his head. No, his reflex was always to protect his face. Only this time, with the speed and force at which the ball was coming at him, when his hands went up, so did his shield. The ball bounced off and shot in another direction, still going with the momentum of the guy's shot.

"What did you do that for?" asked Tom, still in shock. Though he was used to being attacked by flying sports balls, and he'd experienced his fair share of attacks on each of his previous visits at Harding, he'd never summoned a shield without bleeding first. What was even more curious is that he'd neither been angry nor scared. Only surprised.

The guy laughed and came over. Tom eyed him warily and flipped open his signet ring in case he needed to fight this new guy. Then he remembered Headmaster Lianon's comments about using all his gifts instead of relying on unstable magic.

The guy was smiling as he approached Tom, extending his hand when he got close enough.

"You must be Tom," he said in a faint British accent Tom couldn't place, his hand outstretched.

Tom stared at the hand, then took a closer look at the stranger's face. He was older, maybe in his early twenties. Tall and muscular, his long black hair was tied back with a rubber band. He couldn't be a student, but he looked too young to be a teacher. Did Harding have Graduate students? Maybe he worked at the school in some other capacity.

"How would you know that?" Tom asked, squinting at the guy whose smile never wavered and whose hand still waited.

"My name is Emmet, I'm new here and I was told there was a new student."

"Are you a student?" Tom asked, still ignoring the hand hovering between them. A normal person would have dropped it by now. Surely, it was a strain on his arm and shoulder, but Tom didn't see a twitch.

"Not exactly," replied Emmet. "But I'm here to teach you, Tom."

Tom knew he was pushing rudeness by not shaking the guy's hand. Not that he'd confirmed his identity, Tom gingerly put his hand out to shake Emmet's. The guy had a firm grip and he held on a little too long for comfort. He was also one of those people who took a step closer and stared you in the eye, waiting for you to flinch or look away. At 6', Tom rarely met anyone who was a lot taller than he was. This guy had to be at least 6'3".

Clearly, this was part of the test. And Tom would not fail, yet again, at a test he didn't know was happening. Tom stared back and said, "nice to meet you, Emmet."

Satisfied, Emmet let go of Tom's hand and took a step back. He stood in what Tom could only describe as a military stance: at ease. Emmet was wearing sweats similar to those Tom wore, but he filled them out. Where Tom was a boy, this was a man.

"Should I call you Sir?" he asked, appalled at his previous rudeness if this was, in fact, a teacher.

"No, Emmet is fine. I'm not a Professor or anything."

"What are you, then? What are you meant to be teaching me?" asked Tom, unnerved by the man's stance and placid face. He looked very different now that he wasn't flashing his pearly whites at Tom. He looked menacing. He looked like he could handle himself in a fight.

"Are you a martial arts teacher?"

Emmet laughed at this. "No, but you look like you might need lessons."

Affronted, Tom blurted, "I'm a blue belt in Brazilian Ju-Jitsu."

Emmet stopped laughing. "Is that so?" he said, changing his stance. *I'm an idiot. This guy can clearly wipe the floor with me.*

"Yes, they taught a class at The Academy called Martial Arts, but it was basically BJJ. You couldn't earn stripes though; I only just got mine last Summer, when I turned sixteen, at my local Academy in Cork," Tom explained.

Emmet nodded. "Tell me, Tom. Why are you here?"

"Here at Harding?"

"No, here in the gym. You clearly didn't come to shoot hoops," said Emmet, a corner of his mouth twitching slightly.

"Yeah, no. I'm not much of basketball player. Or any team sport, really." Tom was debating whether or not to tell Emmet the truth. If he told him he'd come to spar with Arturo, he'd likely offer to spar with him. And while Arturo was one of the school's better Warlocks, Tom got the feeling that Emmet would be an even more challenging opponent.

He settled on a partial truth. "I was looking for Arturo."

Emmet frowned and tapped on his upper lip for a moment before asking, "Is he the one that levitates?"

"Yeah, that's why I came in when I saw you."

"I don't levitate," stated Emmet.

"Well, you paused near the basket to slam the ball through the net," replied Tom.

"I can slow down time, that's how I do it." To demonstrate he jumped up, hovered in mid-air then fell to his feet.

"Wow, that'd be so useful when playing Balancing Board," Tom said, impressed.

"It was. I was Crown Champion every year while I attended Harding."

"You went to school here?"

"Don't look so surprised!" replied Emmet with a chuckle. "It's not like there are loads of Magical Academies to choose from in the UK."

Tom smiled a little and replied, "right!" He had no idea how many Magical Academies there were in the UK, or even around the world. He'd only ever known about The Academy. They learned about other magical humans at school, and of course, they would have to go to school somewhere, but he'd never really paid much attention to it until it was suggested he attend one.

"What did you major in?" Tom asked more out of habit than actual curiosity.

"International Relations," said Emmet.

"Really? That's what I'm majoring in! I was majoring in Global Studies at my old school, which is a wider program," Tom stopped himself before he started to prattle on about something Emmet had already been told about him.

Tom had neither seen nor requested a prospectus. They'd simply told him IR was the best fit for him. Since he'd only started in January, he'd be placed with the Winter term students, and given credit for the exams or papers he'd missed.

"Is that why you're here? To tutor me on what I missed?"

"Not exactly, though I am here to tutor you on skills you will need going further," replied Emmet. Tom didn't miss how Emmet dodged the question, and he was about to ask a clarifying question when Emmet put up his hand.

"I promise I'll answer all your questions in class, on Monday. It's Saturday night, surely you have better things to do."

"Oh, I'm sorry. I didn't mean to keep you," replied Tom. Of course. Emmet probably came to the gym to unwind, taking advantage of the absence of students. With Tom here, he probably wanted to leave and do something else.

"You're not keeping me from anything, but I came here to let off some steam. Is that why you're here too?"

Tom frowned. That's exactly why he'd come down here. But he found now that he was calm and relaxed. The whole incident had distracted Tom from all his other problems. It was refreshing.

"It was, but I feel better now. I guess I only needed a distraction," he said frankly, shrugging.

Emmet was giving him an assessing gaze.

What's he thinking now?

It made Tom nervous, and he absently went to spin his ring. His ring! He wasn't wearing his ring! Had he forgotten to put it back after his shower? No, he remembered slipping it on as soon as he got back to his room. He stared dumbly and his naked thumb. It hadn't slipped off. Someone had taken it. He supposed any number of students could have removed it magically without his knowledge. But surely, he would have felt it missing before now, right?

No, this had only just happened. *Emmet had taken it. When? Why?* Tom was pretty sure he knew how. If Emmet could slow down time, he probably slipped it off his hand when they shook hands.

When Tom looked up, Emmet held his hand, palm facing up. There was Tom's ring. He made a move to retrieve it, but Emmet closed his fingers around it and put a hand up.

"I promise I'll give it back in a moment, when you've answered a few questions."

"It was my Father's. I don't like to be parted with it," Tom said through clenched teeth.

"I know. Just humor me," he said and placed the ring on the floor between them very slowly and took a step back. The ring was now closer to Tom than it was to Emmet, though Tom knew it could be snatched up without him even noticing.

"Ok, fine."

"How do you feel, Tom?" he asked.

"Are you also the school psychologist?" said Tom with a nervous laugh.

Emmet only stared, patiently waiting for an answer.

"I feel fine, thank you," replied Tom, his words only moderately dripping in sarcasm.

Emmet nodded. "How did you feel before you got to the gym? And earlier today? Or for the past week or so?"

Tom looked at him askance, pursing his lips, as he was about to tell Emmet that it was none of his business and he didn't see how this was relevant. But hadn't Tom complained that no one listened to him not thirty minutes ago? Here was someone asking him how he felt. Tom looked over his shoulder at the door to the gym, retracing his steps in his mind. How had he felt before coming to the gym?

Like a kettle ready to whistle.

He looked back at Emmet, his placid expression betraying nothing. How did he feel now?

Great, actually.

"Are you one of those people who can incite calm onto other people?" Tom asked, pointing a finger at Emmet.

"No, but I often wish I had that gift. People in my line of work often need to chill out."

"What line of work is that?"

"You can ask your questions tomorrow. For now, you answer mine. How do you feel?"

Tom sighed. "A little suspicious, but otherwise great."

"And how have you been feeling of late?"

"Like a paranoid git with a short fuse," huffed out Tom. It was true. He'd been wound up so tightly, it was a wonder he hadn't blown up.

"Ever since I got my powers..." Tom started, but Emmet cut him off.

"Have you been an angry paranoid git since August?" he asked.

Tom narrowed his eyes at Emmet. The man knew entirely too much about him.

"No. I was tense and more than a little restless, but not paranoid,"

Tom said, trying to pinpoint exactly when he'd started acting crazy. "I guess it started after the showdown with The Master," Tom said.

"Did The Master touch you or come into contact with any of your things," asked Emmet.

Realization dawned on Tom. "He took my Key, but I got it back. He didn't have time to curse it or anything."

"What about the ring?" inquired Emmet.

Tom frowned and scratched his head. "The ring came off while I was fighting a Warlock. The Master was nowhere near us and the Warlock," Tom paused and took a deep breath, "died almost right away. So, he couldn't have cursed it."

"The ring is cursed, that's for sure," Emmet said, nodding at the ring.

"How do you know?"

"You've met Miss Clementine, right?" Tom nodded. "She reads your memories when she holds your hand. When I hold your hand, I read, well, evil."

"Evil? Are you saying I'm evil?" Tom shouted. Dread was forming in the pit of his stomach like bilge water rising. Emmet had named the one thing that lurked at the back of his mind: Blood Magick made him evil.

That's why The Master wants me so bad. He thinks we're kindred spirits.

"No, I don't think you're evil, and I didn't *sense* that you're evil either. But I could feel the evil in the ring and so I slipped it off your thumb and placed it in a secure pouch that I always carry with me. It's lined with iron filings."

Tom knew iron was known to ward off ghosts and other malevolent entities. Why Emmet needed to carry a pouched lined in iron on his person was just another question to add to Tom's ever-growing list.

"I held it for only a moment, just now, and I wanted to clog myself over the head. I can't imagine how you managed to wear it for nearly two weeks."

Tom had stopped listening; he was trying to recall the last two weeks since the attack and the more he tried, the fuzzier everything became. If there had been a chair, he'd have sat down. But he was too self-conscious to just drop to the floor and sit with his arms wrapped around his knees.

Lola and Devlin had been right. The Headmaster had been right. Even his mom and Arabella had tried to reason with him. And he'd acted like a monster. He had to apologize. To everyone.

"I...Everyone tried to tell me that I had changed, and I just thought they were trying to control me. I've been such an ass..." Tom said running his hands through his hair.

"Don't beat yourself up. I don't think you were supposed to find out."

"But how did he do it?"

"My guess is The Master had a replica made and swapped out the ring while you were otherwise engaged. Is that possible?" asked Emmet.

Tom nodded, remembering. "Yes, the Warlock grabbed my hand when...when I stabbed him. I thought he was trying to keep his balance, but I now realize my ring may have been his only goal." The truth of it sank in and with it, Tom staggard back until he felt for a wall to lean against.

"He wasn't even trying to hurt me; just steal my ring. I killed him," he said as tears welled up in his eyes, the pain and guilt oozing up his throat and constricting it until he could no longer speak.

Emmet approached Tom slowly, like he would a shelter dog. When Tom didn't bolt or recoil, he came closer and placed a hand on his shoulder. "It was an accident, Tom. You have to forgive yourself."

Once Tom had regained his composure, Emmet suggested they spar on the mats. No magic, just martial arts. Emmet was a brown belt and Tom had his ass handed to him on more than one occasion. When they were through, Tom needed another shower. And though he was sure he'd feel sore in the morning, he hadn't felt this good in weeks. Before he left the gym, he needed to ask Emmet about his ring.

"Do you mind if I take it to Professor Montague to see if we can 'uncurse it'?" Emmet beat him to the subject.

Tom chewed the inside of his cheek. The last time he'd lost sight of his ring, there had been dire consequences.

"I don't know....It's a family heirloom and I feel kind of naked without it. I know I can't wear it, but do you think I could hold on to it? In the pouch, I mean. I have a class with Professor Montague tomorrow and I promise to let her have a look at it."

It was Emmet's turn to hem and haw. "It's only that there's a faculty meeting after dinner and I thought it would be important to update everyone on this latest development."

Tom was grateful to Emmet for easing his burden. Not only had he ended Tom's paranoia and generalized hopelessness, but he'd also given Tom a shoulder to cry on, so to speak. Besides, his powers were very cool, and Tom had caught himself more than once wishing he had an older brother like Emmet.

"Sure, why not," he said finally and left the gym lighter in more ways than one.

CHAPTER

SIXTEEN

WHEN TOM WENT DOWN to breakfast the next day, he didn't see any of his friends. He hadn't seen them last night when he got back to the common room. Either they'd gone home for the weekend, or they came in after he was asleep and weren't up yet.

He didn't feel like meeting anyone new so early on a Sunday morning. Well, early by teenage standards. It was nine. The meals at Harding were all cafeteria-style; you got a tray, stood in line, and sat wherever you wanted. Tom imagined this was how it was in most universities.

The food was okay, but nowhere near the five-star gourmet level it was at The Academy. He'd have to warn Lola when she came for her Summer classes; she was a total foodie. Lola. He needed to see her. Could he just show up, and beg her forgiveness? Surely, she and Devlin would understand.

He finished eating and wandered the school. He'd brought his schedule with him so he could locate his Monday classes. When he'd been here the last time, he'd been shadowing Mandy. And he'd spent a lot of time with Professor Montague.

There were students here and there as he made his way down the stone halls. Out of their robes, they looked like regular teenagers. Most of them were older than Tom. Since he'd crammed his senior year into a semester, he was at least a year younger than most first years. If it hadn't been an emergency, he wouldn't have started until the Fall term.

There was a map at the back of his schedule, and Tom turned right to reach the north wing. He had quite a few classes in this part of the school; though there was no telling what they were since they were identified by a code. The hall led to an outer door. When he opened it, he saw a covered path, connecting the two buildings. He ran. It was freezing, and he hadn't brought a coat or sweater.

He paused to read the plaque on the door: *Harding Preparatory Academy*. It was too cold to puzzle it out. He tried the handle and the door opened.

Rubbing his hands for heat, he kept going, checking his map. The classrooms were closer together. When he peeked through the windows, he saw neat rows of about twenty desks and chairs.

This looks a lot like high school.

He located four of the rooms. Each had the name of the class written by hand on a piece of colored cardboard with the name of the teacher: Potions and Alchemy with Professor Filigree, Defensive and Offensive Magic with Professor Hilltop, Spellcasting with Professor Montague, and History of Magic with Professor Bellamy.

Tom had met all but the History Professor, on the day he had the death bracelets that no one could get off. He shivered at the recollection; While everyone was panicking, Tom had been blissfully asleep, unaware that his life was slowly slipping away.

As luck would have it, Professor Bellamy's door was open. He paused in front of it. Tom poked his head in and immediately regretted it. The elderly Witch was at her desk, presumably grading papers, and spotted him. In a flash she was ushering him inside, offering him tea and biscuits, and asking about his life story.

There was no way out of it. It's not like he had anything better to do. And the cookies were good. This classroom was arranged differently; instead of neat rows, the desks formed a circle. There was no blackboard and Tom imagined it was like The Academy; the teachers' words were dictated onto giant suspended parchments and were erased when the invisible quill reached the bottom of the page. Tom had learned to take notes quickly early on.

When Tom asked about the seating arrangement, the teacher replied, "I was blessed with the gift of illusion." Tom waited for more, but apparently, it was meant to be self-explanatory. Tom thought back to his birthday party. Yvan, the illusionist, could make anyone see anything, anytime. He'd made a group of 20 kids think they were in a secret underground Speakeasy, while they were, in fact, in a plain 15-feet canopy tent.

"Are you saying you take the students back in time to see the events you are teaching about?" he asked, enthusiastic about a history class for the first time in his life.

"It's not *Time Travel*, but you could say the students are transported to another time," she replied dreamily, as though saw an entirely different scene in her own mind.

Tom didn't know if he should say anything, so he ate his cookies and drank his tea. He didn't have any grandparents, and he imagined this was how it felt like to visit one's granny. She would tell him stories about the past and feed him treats.

He was chuckling quietly to himself when Professor Bellamy placed her hand on his upper arm, and he joined her in the vision. It was like being a ghost, an invisible observer; there, but not there. Tom thought this might be what it felt like to astral project. He'd have to ask Lola. *Lola.* He needed to call her.

The Professor's arm threaded through Tom's, and she was standing next to him. They were outside, here at the castle, on a warm sunny day. It was amazing that he could feel the warmth of the sun, hear the surf beyond the cliffs, and smell the heady aroma of pink Daphnes.

They strolled arm in arm for a while until they stopped in front of a group of students, seated cross-legged, holding hands, eyes closed. The students looked about thirteen or fourteen, and their teacher was unmistakable: it was a much younger version of Professor Bellamy.

"How long ago was this?" he whispered, knowing the very old Witch might take offense, but he had to know.

Either she didn't care or was too polite to rebuke him on their adventure.

"They can't hear us, dear. This was nearly a century ago." She led him halfway around the circle and stopped. She pointed at a boy, "That's Dermot Callahan, your great, great, great uncle."

Tom peered at the boy, looking for a resemblance between them but found none other than they both had dark hair. As he studied the boy, he noticed there was something familiar about him but couldn't quite put his finger on it. He wondered if perhaps he looked like someone he'd seen in the old photographs in his father's study. That was probably it, and he let it go.

The scene had changed. They were back in the classroom, but not in Tom's time. Students were seated on straight wooden chairs with handheld slates in their laps. It occurred to Tom that the slates were about the size of today's tablets and were likely called tablets back in the day.

Again, Professor Bellamy pointed at a student, a girl this time. "That's Maeve Callahan, Dermot's daughter and your great, great aunt." The girl was fair with dark hair. Tom would have bet her eyes were green and haunting. She looked like a porcelain doll, the kind whose eyes rolled back in her head and gave you the creeps. He shuddered at the image and shifted his weight.

Another scene change, this time in a cafeteria, but not the one he'd eaten at this morning. This was probably the secondary school cafeteria. Professor Bellamy was older, though not quite as old as she was now. She was standing next to a man in his forties that looked a lot like his dad.

"Da!" he called out. It was futile. They could not hear them. And it wasn't his father. His father was a Traveler and had never attended Harding Academy. Besides, judging by the old radio, and the simple, plain food on the table, this scene must have happened in the 1960s.

"No, dear," said the teacher. "I'm sorry, I should have warned you. That was Brian Callahan, your granduncle."

"He looks like he could have been my grandfather!" Tom blurted out. He took a step closer, but the teacher had brought them back to the present.

"That's because there had been twins. Your grandfather was Brendon Callahan," she explained.

"I was told that he died when my father was a child. Did he go to school here?"

Professor Bellamy's eyes shifted to the right and her smile faltered for the briefest of instants. "No dear, not that I'm aware of." It was a cryptic answer, but before Tom could ask any follow-up questions, she had one of her own.

"Did you have a lot of extended family growing up? Aunts, uncles, cousins? Grandparents on your mother's side perhaps?" she asked between sips of tea. Tom took a sip, thinking the tea would be cold, but it was still warm, like no time had passed while they'd gone into the past.

"Just my Uncle Aidan, Mam's brother, and he never married or had kids. Their parents died before I was born. My parents had a lot of Traveling friends, who Tabitha and I called aunt and uncle, but we weren't related or anything."

He often wished he'd had cousins like Keith had. Though Keith bemoaned the frequent visits of his annoying cousin Bernie, he'd often shared hilarious stories from their shared childhood. Keith was as close to having a brother, or cousin, as Tom could get. Tom was ashamed that he'd pushed Keith away when he first got his powers, thinking his best friend would blab to everyone. There was another apology to put on his list. He'd need a toolbelt for all the fences he needed to mend.

The Professor was saying something. "I'm sorry, Professor. I was woolgathering; could you repeat that?"

"I asked if you were quite alright. I hope I didn't upset you," she said, a slight frown creasing her papery skin.

How old is she?

Tom remembered from his Magical Beings class at The Academy that Witches could live up to three hundred years, though the average was about one hundred and seventy-five in modern times.

"I'm fine. I was only thinking about how lovely it would have been to have aunts and uncles and cousins. It was just Arabella and me." At the Professor's crestfallen expression, he quickly added, "we had a lot of friends in the Traveling Community."

She merely nodded and glanced at the wall clock. Tom took this as his cue to leave. He wondered if he should shake her hand, or bow, or something to show his respect. She really was a wonderful old lady.

In the end, he chose to incline his head as he thanked her for the tea and cookies, and for the blast from the past.

"It was my pleasure, young man. Come back anytime!"

"Thank you. I'm looking forward to class on Monday," Tom said and found he was indeed very eager to return. Not only would her class be highly enjoyable, but Tom had a feeling she would be a fountain of useful information.

CHAPTER

SEVENTEEN

TOM FOUND his other classrooms easily enough in the main building. They'd arranged his morning classes to be in the north wing while his afternoon classes were major-specific. It would make it easier to travel back and forth; he'd be sure to wear an extra layer in the morning.

Though he'd been given a tour by Mandy when he'd first visited, Tom gave himself another tour, extending his visit now to the third and fourth floor. There was a fifth, but the doors were locked, and it was off-limits to students.

When he got back to the main quad, it was time for lunch. There was no sign of friends as he scanned the cafeteria. They had probably gone home for the weekend. It occurred to Tom that he didn't need to stay on campus. He could easily use a Door to and from school every day. Which would have been a great solution had the atmosphere at home been even remotely appealing. Or even if it had been safe to do so.

Nonetheless, when Tom finished eating, he dropped his tray and left the cafeteria, intent on going home for an hour or so to update his mom on what had been happening. If she was home, she would be happy to see him.

He went straight to the main entrance and walked out. The frigid late March coastal breeze assaulted him, and he berated himself again for not dressing warmer.

I'm not at The Academy anymore in a temperature-controlled bubble.

He took out his Key and went home through his Door. All was quiet at the London flat. A quick tour of the place confirmed neither his mother nor his sister were home. He should have known they'd be off galivanting with their respective friends, now that the restrictions for them to move around had been lifted.

Tom checked his watch. It was a little after one-thirty, making it nine-thirty in Virginia. Lola would be up, and Tom knew the whole family were early birds. He decided to chance a surprise visit. If he called, there was a good chance Lola, or Devlin for that matter would refuse to see him.

He summoned his Door again and exited outside the Evers' front door. Deja Vu. He rang the bell and was relieved that Lola herself answered the door. She looked happy to see him at first, then seemed to recall she was angry with him and rearranged her face in an unconvincing scowl.

She's adorable.

This was a good sign. She didn't want to be at odds with him. Truth be told, Lola didn't like being at odds with anyone, always playing peacemaker between arguing parties. Still, she made to close the door in his face.

"Lola, hear me out. You were right. You and Devlin and Headmaster Lianon were right about me. I changed."

She narrowed her eyes at him, stepped aside, and nodded at him to come in.

So far so good.

She looked back and up, toward the staircase. Tom was pretty sure she wasn't inviting him to her room. He'd only seen her room once, in a quick tour of the house, with Devlin shadowing their every move. No, she was likely calling her brother down via telepathy. True enough, Devlin came racing down the steps, his eyes trained on Tom as though getting ready for a fight.

Lola held a hand up. "He's here to explain. I think we should listen."

"Tom," said Devlin, crossing his arms in his usual protector pose.

"Devlin," replied Tom, flashing one of his winning smiles to no effect.

"Shall we sit in the parlor?" asked Lola, gesturing to the right and making a very convincing imitation of a proper southern hostess. Tom nodded and followed her down the hall and into the parlor.

She chose one of the single armchairs and Devlin rushed in to take the other. Tom sat alone on the sofa, awkwardly facing his interrogators. Tom was nervous and didn't know where to start. He was fiddling with his fingers, acutely aware of the absence of his father's ring.

That's a great place to start.

He put up his hand to show them. "I'm not wearing my ring."

They frowned and looked at one another. Tom kept talking.

"You see, it was switched during my altercation with The Master. He cursed it. It was making me crazy, angry, paranoid. Everything you said I was, but I couldn't see it."

Lola's facial expression was the first to soften. Devlin only lifted his chin, as though saying "I'm going to need more information."

"How did you find out?" Lola asked, scooting to the edge of her seat to peer at him in concern.

Tom smiled and let go of the breath he'd been holding. She believed him. The relief made him almost giddy.

"Harding hired a tutor of some sort for me, and I met him in the gym last night by chance," Tom began. "He has two of the coolest powers I've ever heard of. He can slow down time, and he can sense evil by touch."

Devlin's brow went up at this and the scowl disappeared from his face. Tom may not be out of the woods yet, but Devlin was interested in what he had to say.

"What do you mean by 'sense evil by touch'?" asked Devlin.

"He said that if he holds or shakes someone's hand, he can feel if they are evil," replied Tom.

"And he thought you were evil?" shrieked Lola, a hand flying to cover her mouth.

Tom hung his head. "It's what I thought at first, too. I mean, the thought of being evil because I had Blood Magick was always present at the back of my mind. But no, he said he sensed the evil coming from the ring."

"But how can someone curse a ring while you're wearing it?" asked Lola.

"I lost it during the struggle with the Warlock," replied Tom, hoping neither of them would press him for more details. "It was off my finger for no more than fifteen minutes. I found it on the floor just before I went through the Portal with Headmaster Lianon."

Devlin looked at Lola and she only shook her head. Tom hated it when they had these silent conversations. He wished he was party to whatever they were saying.

"And you think that's when the ring was cursed?" asked Lola.

"I don't know. The Master could have cursed a replica of the ring and switched it out when I was distracted," replied Tom. He didn't like keeping secrets from Lola, or Devlin for that matter, but he was afraid of how she'd look at him when she found out he'd killed a man.

"Emmet, the tutor, took it to Professor Montague so she can examine and see if it can be uncursed. I'll know more about it tomorrow. I just wanted to let you know."

"It's a good thing this tutor caught it; there's no telling how bad it would have gotten if you'd continued to wear the ring," said Lola, a shudder going through her body at the thought.

Devlin was still frowning. Tom could see he had more questions, but he did not voice them. "Yes, you're very lucky."

Lola got up and went to sit next to Tom on the sofa, putting an arm around him as she kissed his cheek. "I'm glad you're back to your old self. I was really worried about you," she said and rested her head against his arm. Tom felt the swell of emotions rise within him. His eyes stung and his throat constricted; he couldn't speak. He looked at Devlin who shifted uncomfortably in his seat before rising.

"I will go check on the twins," he said and left the room without waiting for a reply.

Tom lifted his arm and drew Lola to his side. When she snuggled into him and sighed, he placed a soft kiss on the top of her head and just held her. And just like that, all was right with the world.

CHAPTER

EIGHTEEN

TOM AND LOLA spent the morning together and he stayed over for lunch. It was just like the date that he thought they'd have the day before; they watched a movie, made out on the couch, and talked about the future. A few times, he thought about telling Lola about the blood spear and the Warlock, but he just wasn't ready. The fewer people who knew, the better.

Instead, Tom told her more about his meeting with Emmet and visiting the past with Professor Bellamy. Sure, it wasn't the same as Time Walking like they'd done with Professor Ballantyne, but it had been fun. And Lola agreed that the old Witch would likely prove to be a fountain of information.

All too soon, it was time for Tom to go back to school. Students were expected back in the dorms by eight p.m. on Sunday nights to ensure they had a good night's rest. Tom was looking forward to seeing his new friends, too.

"I had a great time, Tom. Thanks for coming over. You were right, we needed to spend time away from school and all the recent drama," said Lola, arms around his waist and looking up at him.

She was just so adorable. Tom couldn't resist kissing the tip of her nose. She laughed and wiped her nose on his shirt. "That tickles!"

"Promise me we won't let this stuff come between us again," Tom said, serious now. "I know I was an ass, and I should have believed you when you tried to make me see reason. It's clear now, but it was so hard to see, just a haze of denial and some awful inability to face reality. Maybe we should have a code word."

"What, like if I say watermelon in the middle of a conversation. Then you'll know you're being an idiot?" she said, giggling at the thought.

"Or I could say squirrel when I feel like you're overreacting," replied Tom. Lola swatted the back of his head playfully. "You're on!"

"I can't promise to write every night this week, but we could check in with each other mid-week. To make plans for next weekend, okay?" Tom knew Lola liked to plan things. She would like this plan. And he wasn't wrong. She rose on tiptoes, bracing herself on his shoulders and kissed him.

"That sounds great, Tom. Now go on before you get into trouble," she said.

Tom checked his watch. It was weird that he'd had lunch twice today but would be skipping dinner altogether due to the time difference. He squeezed Lola one more time and kissed her until her legs started to buckle.

"TOM! WHERE HAVE YOU BEEN?" asked Benny when Tom walked into the common room. He was sitting with a bunch of people, including Mandy and Zaina.

"I could ask you guys the same thing," he said, plopping down on the well-worn leather sofa next to Mandy. "I've been here all weekend."

"We went home, of course!" Benny replied.

The ever-cheerful Mandy's face fell. "Are you not allowed to go home on weekends?" she asked.

"No, it's just that I've spent more than enough time with my family over Spring break and I thought I might hang out with you guys, instead," replied Tom.

"Sorry, dude. But we spend enough time at school during the week. Some of us have lives!" put in Zaina.

"Oh? What shenanigans were you up to then?" asked Benny, drumming his tented fingers and pumping his eyebrows.

Tom was eager to find out what Zaina did in her spare time. He was also surprised that the gang didn't spend time together away from school. He knew most of his Academy friends hung out on weekends and he'd always been miffed at missing out because he was underage.

As far as Tom knew, Benny, Zaina, and Mandy were over eighteen and had met at the beginning of the Fall term.

"My older sister came home for the weekend. She had a row with her boyfriend, which is sad, but I hadn't seen her since the Holidays. We went shopping, had sushi at a new place in Glasglow, ..." Explained Zaina before Tom interrupted.

"You live in Glasglow?" he asked. Only realizing now that he'd never thought to ask where his new friends were from.

"Yeah. Where did you think I lived?" she asked, eyes narrowing.

"I had no idea. It's just you have a British accent...," said Tom. To be honest, he was expecting her to say she was from somewhere in the Middle East. With her dark curly hair and even darker eyes, he was unsure of her heritage.

"Oh, right. I forget. My Mom's a diplomat so we tend to move around."

Anxious to change the subject, Tom asked another question that he was now burning to ask.

"How do you get home?" he asked, looking first at Benny, then Zaina, ending with Mandy.

"Benny, where do you live? Mandy, you said you were American. Do you live in the UK, then?"

Benny answered first. "I'm from London, born and raised in Richmond. As to how we go home, it's not as convenient as your Door, but we use Portal tokens."

At Tom's confused expression, Mandy piped in. "I live in Vermont, near the Canadian border. Portal tokens," she said, and took out a copper coin from her pocket to show Tom, "are enchanted and given to students so they can travel between home and school."

Tom took the coin. It was a little larger than a two-bit euro coin, but not as heavy. There was the Harding Academy crest on one side, and Mandy's name on the other. He gave it back to her.

"But it only works twice per week at specific times: between four and eight on Fridays and Sundays. If we get sick and need to go home, or if we've forgotten a textbook, then we need to call the school and request a special pass," added Zaina.

"So, no ditching school?" asked Tom, with a chuckle.

"Not until *you* arrived," replied Zaina, rubbing her hands together like she was hatching an evil plan.

Tom put his hands up in protest. "I was just kidding! I've never ditched school before, and I'm not about to start now. Besides, I'm pretty sure they're keeping a close watch on me."

When he was in regular high school, he would never have dared. His father would have given him one of those lectures that are so much worse than being shouted at. The fear of ever disappointing his dad had kept him on the straight and narrow. Once he was at The Academy, the question was moot because they couldn't leave the pocket world during the week.

"How does it work?" he asked.

Benny got up and stood in the middle of the seating area. He took out his own coin and threw it out in front of him like he was throwing it in a fountain. It went about four feet before it seemed to hit an invisible wall that morphed into a circular Portal, very much like the ones the High Elves used. It was round and covered with a water-like shimmer. When Benny went to cross, the barrier wouldn't let him, and he was pushed back.

"See? It won't let me pass," said Benny. He extended his hand and waited a moment. The Portal spun inward and shrunk until it was the size of the coin and dropped into Benny's palm.

"That is so cool!" Tom said. "Do you want to see how my Key works?"

Everyone laughed and Tom wondered if he'd missed a joke. Mandy put a hand on his thigh and said, "Sorry to be the one to break it to you, Tom, but you're not the first Traveler to grace these halls."

"But you *are* the first Blood Mage anyone has ever seen!" said Benny before adding, "I can't wait to see what else you can do!"

"You and me both, Benny," Tom replied with a smile.

"So, tell us, Tom. What made you take the plunge?" asked Zaina. Seeing Tom's blank expression, she added, "Switch schools. You seemed pretty attached to your girlfriend and her Swedish brother."

The way she said it sounded a little judgy to Tom's ears and he looked at Zaina's face to see if her expression matched her tone. She wore a pleasant smile, too pleasant to be anything but sarcasm. Any minute now, Tom imagined she might start to bat her eyelashes at him to prove her innocent intentions.

This girl has bite.

They were all looking at him, awaiting his answer. It was obvious, wasn't it? He needed to gain knowledge and skills to defeat The Master and a school for Travelers wasn't going to cut it. Tom got the feeling that's not what his friends wanted to hear.

"In the end, it came down to where I felt most supported. When I was attacked at Harding, you guys had my back, and I won't ever forget that."

Just then, Marvin, their den mother, stuck his head in and told them to scatter. "Lights out in thirty minutes."

"That's right! I'm glad you know who your real friends are," said Benny, clapping Tom on the back as they made their way to their rooms.

"You guys! We're like the Four Musketeers!" said Mandy in a singsong voice. "Come on, group hug!"

She was waving her hands in the air, motioning them to come on. Benny grabbed Tom's arm and pulled him toward Mandy. When Zaina made a beeline for her room, Benny froze her in place.

"Benny, I swear to God, if you don't unfreeze me right now, I'm going to tie you to your bed all night with the Golden Ropes. See how you like peeing yourself in the morning," said Zaina through gritted teeth. Though her body was frozen, she could still talk through her partially open lips.

"Just a sec, Zaina," said Benny, pulling the other three around Zaina for the group hug. As soon as they were joined, he unfroze her. She pushed at them halfheartedly and barked, "Get off me you weirdos!"

Everyone laughed and dispersed to get ready for bed.

CHAPTER
NINETEEN

TOM GOT DRESSED and added the things he'd need for his morning classes to his backpack. He didn't forget to slip in a sweater.

At breakfast, his friends ribbed him for having to take high school level classes every morning.

"I forget you're new to this magic stuff," said Benny. "You'll love Professor Bellamy."

Tom explained that he'd met the old Witch the previous day while searching out his classrooms.

"Don't eat the sweets on Professor Filigree's desk, advised Mandy. "They taste horrible, and most of them will earn you a trip to the bathroom."

"Duly noted. Thanks for the heads up. What is Professor Hilltop like as a teacher? I only saw him once when he tried to remove the cursed bracelets."

"Don't ask stupid questions and you'll be fine," said Zaina between mouthfuls of cereal.

"How would you describe a stupid question?" asked Tom, tongue-in-cheek.

"That's a stupid question," replied Zaina, giving Tom a stony stare as she resumed eating.

"What Zaina means, is that you should always check your notes or the textbook before asking him a question, or he'll think you're not paying attention and get very angry," said Mandy.

"Will he turn me into a toad?" asked Tom, chuckling at his own joke.

"He could!" replied Benny. "But likely he'll just give you detention."

"Detention! I've never gotten detention. What's that like? Do you copy lines on a piece of paper?" Tom asked.

"Worse! He has you take dictation for him. He's been writing his memoirs for years now and can't be bothered to learn how to use a computer, or even write it down on paper. So, he dictates his life story to the poor unsuspecting students who incur his wrath," explained Benny, rubbing his hand as though he'd only just returned from the teacher's office.

"Gotcha!" said Tom. He scanned the room, looking for Arturo.

"Who are you looking for," asked Zaina.

"Arturo. I haven't seen him since I found out I was transferring schools."

"He's probably holding court in the quad," replied Zaina, rolling her eyes.

"What classes do you have this afternoon? Any chance I might see you guys?" asked Tom, changing the subject before Zaina started on her vendetta against Arturo. Even though Arturo had come through for Tom during the attack, she wasn't ready to cut him any slack. Tom, for his part, was hoping to make a friend out of Arturo, now that he'd earned the older student's respect.

"Afternoon classes are major-specific," said Mandy. "I'm majoring in Biochemistry and Pharmacology, so I have a Cell Biology class this afternoon."

Tom stared at Mandy open-mouthed. "Wow, you must be really smart, then!"

Mandy laughed and tossed her long honey-blond hair over her shoulder. "More than just a pretty face, huh?" Tom could only nod. He'd pegged her as an English major. Turning to Benny, he asked, "How about you?"

"Nothing quite so impressive, I'm afraid. I'm majoring in Film Studies. Monday's class is about debates in film theory," said Benny.

"I have no idea what that means," said Tom, shaking his head and laughing nervously.

"Basically, it's about how pop culture and world culture influence trends in moviemaking."

That didn't make things any clearer, so Tom said, "Okay, good luck with that!"

Tom turned to ask Zaina, but she beat him to it.

"What are *you* majoring in?" she asked.

"International Relations," replied Tom. "Monday's class is very unoriginally titled: Introduction to International Relations," said Tom, reading off his schedule. "Your turn, Zaina."

She gave him a rueful grin and replied, "Guess!"

Tom knew that was a trap. No matter what he said, she was bound to be offended. He looked to Mandy, hoping for a clue, but the girl lifted her hands up as if to say, 'you're on your own'!

Benny was shaking his head. "I'm not saying a word."

Tom thought back to what he'd learned about Zaina until now. She was one of the best Balancing Board players at school, so she was fit, fast, and agile. She had what apparently was a rare power to wield magical artifacts and weapons. To master those, she must have had to do a lot of reading. She was smart and brave, that was a given. From what she'd said about her sister's visit, she was loyal and, despite appearances, knew how to let loose once in a while.

Tom leaned back in his chair and put his hands behind his head as he checked the ceiling for revelations. There were none. He tried to picture her in various academic pursuits: in a white lab coat, in a gym, in an art studio, in a heated debate - she'd be good at that. When enough time had passed that his friends started telling him to just take a wild guess, Tom took a deep breath and said, "Archeology."

He'd expected everyone to start laughing, but it was crickets.

"How did you come up with that?" asked Zaina.

Tom blushed. If he hadn't guessed right, he had to be close. She wasn't angry, for one. In fact, she looked a little stunned.

"Well, you said your family moved around a lot. I assumed that means you've traveled quite a bit and likely speak a few languages. Honestly, the image that came to mind when trying to describe you as a female Indiana Jones, or better yet, Lara Croft."

That got them all in stitches. "Lara Croft? You think I look like Lara Croft?" Zaina asked, obviously offended.

"She's HOT!" put in Benny which got him a murderous look from Zaina.

"And she's a badass!" piped in Mandy.

Though Tom was amused, he could see that Zaina was not. "I didn't say you looked like Lara Croft, I said I pictured you as the female equivalent of Indiana Jones, and Lara Croft is the only one I know. It's not about looks, it's about your mad skills!"

Somewhat mollified, Zaina made an exaggerated pouty face and said, "Well, you were right. I *am* majoring in Archeology." Then, she perked up and added, "My Monday class is called Artefacts and Materials and it's fascinating!"

The bell rang before she could expand. Everyone scattered to different parts of the school. Tom walked through the quad to get to his class, hoping to catch sight of Arturo. The quad was empty, and Tom hurried so he wouldn't be late.

THERE WERE four fifty-minute classes in the morning. The same four classes appeared on Tom's schedule every day but changed timeslots throughout the week. On Mondays, his first class was Defensive and Offensive Magic with Professor Hilltop.

Tom arrived at his first Defensive and Offensive Magic class a few minutes early. He walked into the room and saw Professor Hilltop writing something on the chalkboard. Tom sat down in one of the empty seats and waited for class to begin.

The classroom reminded Tom of the Traveling classroom at The Academy: one part was filled with tables and chairs, and another was partitioned and held no furniture at all. Tom expected that's where they'd put things into practice.

As soon as the other students started trickling in, Professor Hilltop turned around and introduced himself. He told the class that they would be learning how to defend themselves against psychic magical attacks.

The first part of the class was spent on defense. Presumably, for Tom's benefit, Professor Hilltop went over the different types of magical attacks and how to block them. Tom was paying close attention, as he hadn't realized there were so many spells that he could use to disarm an opponent. He took copious notes.

The second part of the class focused on offense. Professor Hilltop had students pair up and come to the front of the class to perform various non-lethal offensive spells. Tom was surprised at how simple some of the spells were. He was reminded of his conversation with Headmaster Lianon and vowed to review the Traveler's Handbook at the earliest opportunity. *Master the skills you already know.*

By the end of class, Tom felt like he had learned a lot. He was looking forward to the next class and trying out the spells he'd learned.

Tom's first class in Potions and Alchemy was definitely an interesting one. Professor Filigree started by teaching them the basics of turning solid objects into sand. Actually, he called it Pulverisation; the output wasn't actually sand. The object was blown into minuscule particles, which pretty much looked like sand. The teacher insisted on providing them with a rather complicated scientific explanation to the point where Tom wasn't sure he would be able to do it. In practice, however, it was actually very straightforward. The key was to produce heat through friction between your hands and surround the object while focusing your magic. After a few tries, Tom finally managed to get the hang of it. This trick would definitely come in handy.

The rest of the class went by in a blur as Tom struggled to keep up with the Professor's explanations. He managed to take some notes, but he was still mostly confused by the end of the class. Overall, though, he thought it was a pretty cool experience and he was looking forward to learning more in future classes.

Next, Tom eagerly entered his first Spellcasting class, which he thought would be easy since he'd taken Spellcasting classes at The Academy. His Latin was decent, and though he'd forgotten a lot of the basic spells from the Handbook, he was sure he'd be able to keep up. Furthermore, Tom was looking forward to finding out what Professor Montague had to say about his ring. He had hoped to ask her as soon as he arrived in the classroom, but she'd been busy with another student.

Professor Montague did not make a fuss about Tom's presence like some of the other teachers had. She acknowledged his presence with a small smile and began today's lesson: the basics of spell assembly, using spells they already knew.

Tom was quickly able to put together a few simple spells and was soon creating complex ones. He made a mental note to bring the Handbook to class tomorrow, as it would come in handy if they were to assemble more spells.

He quickly became one of the top students in the class, much to the surprise of the other students who had been there all year. Once it was revealed that he was a Traveler, the novelty wore off and students resumed worshiping the current star pupil.

When the bell rang, Tom stayed behind and waited by Professor Montague's desk. This wasn't the same room they had used to test Tom's powers. The Professor had seemed quite at ease in the large amphitheater. Perhaps she taught at both levels, and this was the room she used for the high school students.

"What can I do for you, Tom?" asked the Witch when the rest of the students had left.

"I was wondering if you'd had a chance to examine my ring," said Tom, hoping she had not only examined it but also found a way to uncurse it so he could have it back.

Professor Montague's brows knit together, and she gave Tom one of her impatient 'get-on-with-it' looks. When Tom said no more, she asked, "I'm confused, Tom. I examined your ring weeks ago and returned it. Are you saying you've lost it?"

A chill ran down Tom's back. Tom shook his head; he must not have heard her correctly. Or perhaps she had misunderstood him. She was old, after all. He spoke a little louder the second time.

"Professor Montague, Emmet took my ring yesterday and said you would examine it and, if possible, find a way to uncurse it," said Tom, clearly enunciating every word.

"Merciful heaven, Tom. *What* are you talking about? Who is Emmet? Why would your ring be cursed? And *why* are you shouting?"

The questions came at Tom in rapid succession and with increasing volume. He'd annoyed Professor Montague.

"Perhaps I should start at the beginning," said Tom.

"Perhaps you should," replied the Professor.

Tom recounted how he'd found Emmet in the gym and all that had transpired since. Though she was often short with Tom, Professor Montague was one of the people that Tom had learned to trust. Tom gave her a full account of Sunday's activities, including his visit to see Lola and Devlin.

"Tell me what happened with the ring that day at your house. Headmaster Lianon never mentioned anything was amiss with your ring," she asked. She was seated at her desk and had started taking notes in a small, leather-bound notebook.

"When I was fighting the Warlock, he grabbed onto my hand to keep from falling. As he stumbled back, the ring went with him. I forgot about the ring while I was trying to save him, but just before the Headmaster pushed me through the Portal, I saw it on the floor and picked it up."

The Professor's hand was flying across the page. Tom paused to let her finish her notes. "I see," she finally replied.

"And are you certain the one you picked up was indeed your ring? Could it have been replaced by another, identical ring?" she asked, looking straight at him.

He'd never considered that it might not have been his ring. It looked the same and felt the same. No, wait, it *hadn't* felt the same.

"It looked the same to me. But now that you ask, I just remembered something. I kept spinning it on my thumb when I was nervous or anxious. I had never done that before. For one, because it never occurred to me to do so. For another, the ring fit snugly before. I assumed I'd lost weight due to the stress of it all."

"Yes. That is a reasonable assumption. Tell me again how you felt and how you acted while you wore the ring since being parted with it."

Tom's stomach grumbled and he apologized. It was the lunch break, and this was taking longer than he'd anticipated. As though reading his mind, Professor Montague pulled a wand from the fold of her robe and twirled it over the corner of her desk. A plate of food materialized. It was a plain turkey sandwich with a side of salad. Another twirl of the wand produced a fork, a glass of water, and a napkin.

When Tom just stared at the food, the Professor gestured at it and said, "have at it before your grumbling wakes the Ogre."

Tom had sunk his teeth into the sandwich when what she said registered. "There's an Ogre at school?" he exclaimed once he'd chewed his mouthful enough to speak.

"Of course not!" cackled Professor Montague, pleased with her joke.

Tom refrained from making any remarks and stuffed his face until he'd finished the entire sandwich. While he ate, Professor Montague asked simple questions to which he could reply with yes or no. She verified Emmet's physical description and the powers he'd displayed. She also asked approximate times for when things had happened.

Once he'd finished the salad, drank the water, and wiped his mouth on the napkin, Professor Montague snapped her fingers and all traces of his lunch disappeared.

"Now, then. The only Emmet I know is at least eighty years old. However, from the powers you described, I believe it might be a former student. Though he did not major in International Relations. No, I believe the young man you met is Alistair Callahan, your second cousin."

Tom's mind was reeling. He'd felt a kinship with Emmet, a connection that he'd attributed to their shared interests. He'd looked up to the guy, wished he'd had an older brother just like him. He felt sick to his stomach. Once again, Tom had been played the fool. He'd trusted the wrong person. Or had he. Sure, Emmet had stolen his ring. But if it truly was cursed, then he'd helped him. Hadn't he?

Tom said as much to Professor Montague.

"Without the ring to examine, it's hard to say. You said that everyone around you noticed the change in you. It might very well be the result of a curse. If Emmet, or Alistair, was in on the plan, why take the ring from you? Why pretend to be here to teach you and then disappear?"

Tom had no idea. He rubbed his forehead with the tips of his fingers a few times in the hopes of soothing the headache that was starting to form. He had so many questions swirling in his head. *Second cousin!? Who is this? Why have I never heard of him, let alone met him before?* If this person, whatever his name was, *was* truly a relative, then Tom wanted so much to believe him, to give him the benefit of the doubt that he may be helping in some way. Tom was growing tired of complicated relationships. Professor Montague eyed him a moment then spun her wand again. A plate of chocolate chip cookies and a cup of coffee appeared.

Tom grabbed a cookie and smiled. "Thanks, Professor." He wasn't much of a coffee drinker, but as he still had an entire afternoon of classes ahead of him, he dunked his cookie in it and drank the whole cup.

"I forget you're still just a boy," said the Witch giving Tom one of her rare indulgent smiles. "Once you've finished your dessert, I want you to go and get some fresh air. I'll discuss the matter with the Head-mistress. She may want to meet with you after class to view your memories. We can ask Professor Bellamy to join us. Between the three of us, we could go back to view the events and see what you might have missed."

"You can do that?" asked Tom and immediately regretted it. Professor Montague was giving him a stony stare as though to say, 'I'm a two-hundred-year-old Witch, I can do anything.'

CHAPTER

TWENTY

TOM HEADED for the cafeteria in search of his friends, but he didn't find them at the table. He wasn't sure how much of the latest developments he should tell them about. Taking Professor Montague's advice, Tom removed his robes, put on his wool sweater, and headed for the back of the castle as he buttoned up his robes again.

The biting wind hit his face full force and it did an even better job of sharpening his senses than the cup of coffee had. He stuffed his hands in his pockets and walked over to the West Tower. His friends weren't there. But Arturo was!

The guy was sitting on the outer steps, alone, with both hands to his mouth, as though he was eating corn on the cob. As Tom drew near, he heard a melody coming from the harmonica. Arturo, intent on his playing, didn't notice Tom until he was in his line of vision. He faltered but kept playing, keeping a wary eye on Tom. Perhaps he worried that Tom would laugh at him.

The song was nice, if a little sad. When Arturo concluded the piece, Tom clapped and made sure to keep his smile as sincere as possible on his face. The last thing he wanted was to offend Arturo and cause the guy to have a knee-jerk reaction that could prove painful, if not deadly.

"That was great," said Tom.

"Thanks. My Nonno taught me when I was young. He left this to me when he died," said Arturo, holding the harmonica in his hand before slipping it into a pocket.

"I'm sorry he died. I never met either of my grandparents. I bet it was nice spending time with him," said Tom, keeping a friendly smile on his face.

Arturo got up from the steps and started to walk, motioning for Tom to follow.

He fell into step with Arturo, and they walked toward the front of the castle in silence for a few minutes.

"I heard you were back. Are you here to stay?" asked Arturo.

"Yes. I've officially transferred," replied Tom, pulling up his hood when they turned the corner and were hit by a gust of the frigid northern wind.

"That's good. There's more to learn here," he said.

Though the conversation was awkward, Tom was happy he'd finally connected with Arturo. He was sure there was more to learn from the older student.

"I've already learned a lot from this morning's classes. They have me doing high school level magic classes in the morning," explained Tom.

Arturo asked about his classes and Professors and gave some advice of his own.

"I haven't seen you at meals or around the common room. Have you been hiding out?" asked Tom when the conversation lulled again.

"No, I switched common rooms after Spring break," he said.

"Why?"

"One of the den mothers left school and they offered me the job. I was next in line," he explained.

"Are you in year two or three?" asked Tom.

"I'm in year two. Technically, you have to be a year three to be a den mother, but there was no one else on the list. Not that many people volunteer."

"There must be some perks, right?" asked Tom.

"There are. I have my own room, and it's a lot bigger than the dorm rooms. I have my own bathroom, and I can eat in my room if I want to."

"Ah, that explains your absence at breakfast," said Tom.

"We have to eat dinner with everybody else, though. And as cool as all that sounds, being the one to tell others to keep it down, to go to bed, or even to get up, doesn't make me too popular."

Tom bit his lip. While Arturo was clearly popular with the girls and the younger students, Tom didn't think he was all that popular with kids his own age to begin with. As he was trying to get on Arturo's good side, he refrained from pointing that out.

They were almost at the front entrance when the bell rang. Tom would need to start wearing a watch if he didn't want to be late for class.

"Come see me after class. I'll be in the library for study hour," said Arturo, pausing near the hall that led to the science wing.

"I might have to see the Headmistress after school. I'll catch up with you if she doesn't keep me until dinner."

"Are you already in trouble, Tom?" asked Arturo, looking somewhat impressed.

Tom blushed and quickly replied, "No, um, it's something about my transcripts," Tom lied. Arturo was cool, there was no doubt about that. But Tom would need to know a lot more about him before he started spilling his secrets. He'd already messed up by hero-worshiping Emmet. He was going to be super chill about Arturo.

Arturo merely shrugged and said, "catch you later, kid."

Ouch.

THERE WAS no time to hunt for his friends. Tom went directly to the classroom on his schedule.

The teacher, a tall redheaded Scotswoman named Professor Anderson, greeted him warmly and gave him a textbook. The classroom was small and held a large boardroom table with about twenty chairs. Tom sat in one of the empty chairs and took out a notebook and pen after checking what the other students had in front of them.

Once everyone had found their seats, Professor Anderson asked everyone to introduce themselves for Tom's benefit while providing information on the topics they'd covered thus far. Tom was relieved to find out they'd covered most of the topics in his classes at The Academy; all but those that pertained to the Magical Community, as only the implications for Travelers had been considered.

When all students had spoken, Professor Anderson pulled a wand from her sleeve and tapped an invisible object in the air. Instantly, an outline for today's lesson appeared before Tom, and notes started to populate on the blackboard in neat script as the Professor began her lecture on Marxism.

Tom enjoyed the class and found his teacher to be competent yet entertaining, a rare combination in Uni Professors. She was also quite pretty and that never hurt. Tom thanked her as he left the class. She called him back and gave him a slip of paper.

"If you have questions, or need extra notes to catch up, those are my office hours. Please don't hesitate. I know how difficult it can be to transfer mid-semester."

"Thank you, Professor," Tom said politely and left. Tom hadn't taken more than three steps down the hall when he heard Professor Anderson calling him back.

He turned and saw her in the doorway.

"I've just received a message from the Headmistress. She'd like to see you in her office."

"Thank you, Professor. I'll go there directly."

CHAPTER
TWENTY-ONE

WHEN TOM ARRIVED at Miss Clementine's office, Professors Bellamy and Montague were already there.

Tom inclined his head and, looking at each Witch in turn he said, "Good afternoon, ladies."

Miss Clementine giggled and invited Tom to sit with them at the table. There were various ritual items in the center of the table: a tall black candle, some wood shavings, petals from flowers Tom could not identify, and other odds and ends.

Tom was nervous. Though he'd enjoyed visiting the past with Professor Bellamy and sharing his memories with Miss Clementine was no different than sharing them with Headmaster Lianon, this was different. This was going back to the scene of the worst day of his life.

Not only would all three Witches see what he had done, he too would witness it. Moreover, he would be plunged back into the horrifying memory of killing a man, a Warlock. A knot started to form in the pit of his stomach. After two days of feeling hopeful, the anxious knowing of what was about to happen felt terrible.

"Don't worry, Tom. We're only going for a quick visit, to see if we can pick up any additional clues you might have missed. Don't be alarmed if you see more than what you remember. The mind likes to play tricks on us. And it retains a lot more of what is going on in a situation than what our feeble brains can recall," explained Miss Clementine.

The Headmistress was on his right, Professor Montague was on his left, and Professor Bellamy was facing him. The Witches joined hands and waited for Tom to do the same.

"I want you to think back to the first time you remember seeing the ring, Tom," said Professor Montague.

Confused, Tom looked at her. "You mean when I received the ring after my father died?"

"No. I mean the first time you saw the ring. Whenever that might be. Take us there in your mind. Miss Clementine will read your memory and share it. Professor Bellamy will take us there. I'm here to amplify and support the circle," explained Professor Montague.

Tom closed his eyes and thought about the ring. He was trying to think back to a time he remembered seeing it, but he was coming up blank. He felt a jolt of electricity through his left hand. Professor Montague had zapped him somehow and he instantly wanted to release her hand. She held on and he recalled a memory. He was playing in his father's study as a boy. He felt a shift, like the drop you would feel traveling between floors in a rickety old elevator.

When he opened his eyes, there they were. Standing in his father's study. Tom saw himself playing with plastic blocks on the floor, assembling what looked like a castle. He looked to be about five or six. Turning his attention to the desk, he saw his father, bent over one of his journals.

"Da!" he said, unable to stop himself. The ladies didn't say a word. Tom knew his dad couldn't hear him.

He was writing steadily with his favorite pen. The one grandad had given him before he died.

Tom tried to peer closer at what his father was writing but couldn't decipher it.

"Come on lad, it's time," said his father to young Tom.

The boy dropped the handful of bricks he was holding and ran around the desk to stand next to his father. John picked him up and set him on his lap. He folded the page he'd been writing on, so the edge fell just short of the middle of the notebook. He neatly pressed the folded edge. He then took the red candle that had been burning and poured a few drops of wax where the edge of the pages met. Slipping off his ring, he gave it to young Tom. Guiding his pudgy fingers to the right spot, the boy pressed the top of the ring into the wax. He blew on it delicately and removed the ring.

"C is for Callahan!" he shrieked with delight, seeing the half-moon indent the ring had left in the wax.

John claimed the ring and slipped it back onto his thumb. "This ring will be yours one day, Tom."

As the boy began to clap, Tom felt himself shift back to Miss Clementine's office.

"What an adorable boy you were, Tom," exclaimed Professor Bellamy. If they'd been closer, Tom was sure she would have pinched his cheeks. He blushed at the compliment but didn't reply.

"Now, take us to when you received the ring," said Miss Clementine. That was easier to conjure up, as it had happened last Summer. This time, the room felt like it was spinning a little as though the table had spun on itself, but when Tom opened his eyes, he saw himself sitting on his bed at home, reading his dad's letter and holding the red velvet box.

They watched Tom wipe a tear with the back of his hand and open the box. He examined the ring for a moment and slipped it on. He moved closer to take note of the ring so he could compare it with the ring he'd been wearing since the altercation with The Master.

The other ladies were also observing the ring, but Professor Bellamy was trying to read the contents of the letter. Tom summarized the contents for her, and they came back to the present.

"Okay, Tom. It's time to take us to the night when you lost the ring," said Miss Clementine, with an apologetic tone in her voice. Tom took a deep breath and closed his eyes. He didn't want to relive the whole thing, and surely it wasn't necessary. But then again, if they saw it all from the beginning, they might understand where Tom was coming from.

It must have been taking too long because Professor Montague zapped him again. Tom jolted back to the task at hand and his mind reluctantly took them to the moment where the Warlock grabbed his upper arm. Viewing it from an outsider's perspective, Tom realized that it was over in minutes. Living through that day felt like a lifetime.

"Can you slow it down, Hilda?" asked Miss Clementine, presumably addressing Professor Bellamy.

The scene started again. The Warlock grabbed Tom's arm. Tom twisted his wrist while his other arm came to push down on the Warlock's hand so he would loosen his grip. But just before Tom could latch on, the blood running down his hand congealed and stretched, expanding into a pointy spear that kept getting longer until it went through the Warlock's middle. Meanwhile, the Warlock reached for Tom's ring. As the Warlock staggered back, the ring slipped off Tom's thumb.

They watched as the Warlock slid down, his blood staining the wall. Meanwhile, Tom fell to his knees and threw up on the rug. He hadn't noticed when it was happening, but as soon as his hands had touched the ground, the spear had dissolved into a puddle of blood. When he sat on his haunches, arms dangling on either side, the puddle of blood followed Tom's movements and crept up his hand and arm and slid back into the wound on his bicep. When the last drop of the wound had closed, not a trace was left.

They watched Tom rush to the Warlock's side and try to staunch the flow of blood pouring from his chest. The Warlock clutched the gaping hole with one hand, but the other lay on the floor half-open. There was Tom's ring.

Moments later, the Headmaster pushed Tom toward the Portal. The ring was on the floor, some two feet away, where Tom picked it up before leaving through the Portal. But when Tom looked back, still watching the vision, the Warlock was still holding the ring. *There were two rings!*

"I think we've seen enough," said Professor Montague gruffly and they were back in Miss Clementine's office. Tom felt a squeeze from both the Witches and gave a small smile, though his eyes were trained on the black candle. He didn't want to look up and see the look Professor Bellamy would be giving him.

He knew it was an accident, even more so now that he had watched the whole thing happen. But it made him feel like a freak, a dangerous, murderous freak of nature. Sure, it was great to be able to heal people. But that thing, that spear, had come out of him. It had assembled from his blood under his, admittedly unconscious, command.

The Master had egged him on to finish, to kill, the Warlock. Only a supreme being should have the power of life and death. Not a sixteen-year-old boy. And certainly not an evil Sorcerer who wanted to take over the world.

When Tom was about to let go of the Witches' hands, they both held on. "Take us to your meeting with Emmet," said Professor Montague. He'd forgotten all about Emmet.

This time the room shifted sideways like they were on a moving train. The scene slowed once again, and Tom was able to see when Emmet had taken the ring. He was fast! Once they viewed the scene in its entirety, Professor Bellamy brought them back and they all let go of each other's hands.

Tom wiped his hands on his thighs. They were clammy and his arms were sore from holding them out for so long.

"That boy's name isn't Emmet," said Professor Bellamy. "It's Alistair. He looks a lot like his grandfather, wouldn't you agree Tom?"

That's where he'd recognized him from. Not from an old picture, it was from his trip to the past.

"I remember thinking he looked familiar. But with the long hair and the British accent, I couldn't place him. You said he was my second cousin. That means our grandfathers were brothers, twins in this instance. Right? When I saw Brian Callahan in the past, he looked exactly like my dad. But Emmet, er, I mean Alistair, doesn't look like my dad at all. Otherwise, I would have seen the resemblance right away," said Tom, more to himself than to the Witches.

"I believe Alistair takes after his mother, Imogene. That's also how he comes by the accent; he was raised in England," said Professor Bellamy. "What I don't understand is how he is connected to all this.

He was always such a nice, thoughtful boy. I just can't imagine him being in league with The Master."

"So, what he said was true, then? He attended school here?" asked Tom, hoping Alistair turned out to be an ally, not an enemy.

"Oh, yes. He was a very bright student. Always on time, very polite, graduated with Honors if I recall," said Professor Bellamy. She seemed to recall quite a bit. Tom wondered if she could flip through the past like you would a streaming service and that's why she could remember things that had happened years ago.

"Yes, I'm stumped as well. Alistair works for the MFO – the Magical Foreign Office. Perhaps he's been in contact with the CEBM, and they requested his assistance," said Miss Clementine, though her face looked doubtful.

"But why would he lie about being here to tutor me? Or the staff meeting? Or take the ring?" asked Tom. It didn't make sense to him. Ultimately, Alistair had done Tom a service by removing his ring. And as they'd established that the ring had no magical or monetary value, the fact that he would abscond with it was intriguing indeed.

"Don't fret, Tom. We'll get to the bottom of this. The important thing is that you are safe and that we know more now than we did before," replied Miss Clementine.

She rose and the others followed suit. Tom jumped to his feet.

"I'll let you know if there are further developments," said the Head-mistress, as she walked Tom out of her office. "Thank you, Miss Clementine. I appreciate you keeping me in the loop. I get anxious when I don't know what's going on."

"I understand, dear. As soon as we know more, I'll send word to you. In the meantime, you may not have tutoring lessons, but I trust you're making full use of all your classes?"

"Oh, yes, Miss. I've learned more in a day at Harding than I ever could at The Academy. I mean, I loved it there. Don't get me wrong. It's just that it wasn't..." Tom trailed off, unable to express what he meant and feeling disloyal to Headmaster Lianon, and his friends.

"It wasn't the right place for you anymore," she supplied. "We're glad to have you with us and we hope we can help you reach your full potential, both academic and magical."

Tom thanked her and left. As he made his way down the hall, he asked a passing student for the time. It was only five. There was still time to join Arturo in the library.

CHAPTER

TWENTY-TWO

IT TOOK a while for Tom to find Arturo. He'd almost given up and sat down at one of the free tables. He had homework to do. The library at Harding was huge and there was no discernable logic to its layout. When Tom would go down what looked like a hallway, he'd come face to face with a window, or even a wall. Once he'd visited each of the many nooks and crannies and took note of a few spots he could come to if he ever wanted a little peace and quiet, he stumbled upon Arturo.

Throwing up his arms, he exclaimed, "there you are!"

Arturo shushed him teasingly and told him to pull up a chair. Tom dropped into it and lay his head on the table. "I just need a five-minute nap." Arturo laughed and set his timer. Tom lifted his head and peeked out from behind his hair. "Did you just set a timer on your watch?"

"You said you needed five minutes. I'll wake you when the time's up," he said straight-faced.

"Fair enough," replied Tom and let his face caress the cool surface of the table.

He woke to Arturo shaking him. "It's been ten minutes, Tom. You said five minutes."

Tom braced himself on the edge of the table and slowly got upright.

He wiped the drool from his mouth. "I can't believe I actually fell asleep," Tom said. He shook his head and rubbed his eyes.

"What are you up to?" Tom asked, peering at the stack of books Arturo had neatly arranged into five piles.

"I'm doing research."

Tom looked at the first pile. The books were about hematology. He wasn't surprised, since he'd seen Arturo heading to the science wing earlier that day.

"Are you studying to be a doctor?" Tom asked.

"Not exactly," said Arturo, engrossed in the enormous book laid out before him.

Tom took the hint and pulled out his own books. He wanted to read the chapters the group had studied earlier in the year on Defensive and Offensive Magic. He opened his textbook and started reading. It was fascinating stuff. He remembered how awed he'd been that first Summer at The Academy, learning Latin, spells, and the history of magic. But this stuff was on an entirely different level.

He knew there were Witches and Warlocks out in the world, but he'd never met any and they'd never studied them or that kind of magic at The Academy. It had always felt kind of unreal to him. Like the sort of thing that happened in movies. But it was real. And he was one of them.

He looked over at Arturo. The guy could control things with his mind and levitate. Levitate! And there he was, absorbed in some medical textbook. Though they were only two years apart in school, Arturo was a man. He had beefy, hairy forearms, broad shoulders, and a five o'clock shadow. Tom was basically hairless, and he shaved the three hairs he had on his chin once per week.

As though sensing Tom's gaze, Arturo looked up from his book. "What?"

"Sorry. I didn't mean to stare. How old are you?" asked Tom.

"I'm twenty. Why?"

"You look older. Do you know a guy named Alistair Callahan?" Tom asked. He hadn't meant to ask; the question just popped out as he was trying to find something to justify being so nosy.

"Why? Is he related to you?"

Arturo was good at turning questions back to the asker. "Yeah, I guess. He's my second cousin. He came to school here and I thought you might have met him before he left."

Arturo thought about it for a minute. "Is he the guy who can stop time?"

"Yes, he is. Is that a rare power?"

"It's not very common, but it's not special if that's what you mean. Like, I can levitate, and everyone is so impressed, but anyone with telekinesis can levitate if they work at it. They just don't. People who can stop time can also move it forward and rewind it too, aka Time Travel. But they rarely develop the gift to its full potential. If I keep working at it, I may even fly one day."

"Are you kidding?" asked Tom. "That is so cool!"

"Why are you all starry-eyed over flying, Tom. You can heal the sick and wounded, bring people back from the dead, and control people with your mind," said Arturo.

"How....how do you know that?" asked Tom. The Master and his minions had alluded to those powers, but no one had yet confirmed it.

Arturo pushed a second stack of books toward Tom. They were all about electromagnetism. He slid the third stack next to it. Those books were about necromancy. The fourth stack was about energy healing. As Arturo positioned the first stack, then the final stack in front of Tom, he said, "have you even done your homework?" The books in the last pile were all about Blood Magick.

The dinner bell rang, and Tom asked what they should do about the books. "Just leave them here, no one comes here, and the librarian won't disturb them."

"What about that big book, what's it about?" asked Tom.

Arturo put a piece of paper on which he'd been taking notes and used it as a bookmark as he closed the massive tome with a thump. He picked up the book and held it so Tom could read the title: Molecular Microbiology.

"So, I guess you're into all of this, right?" asked Tom, pointing at all the books Arturo had clearly taken the time to assemble for him.

"More to you than it would seem," he replied. "Come on, I'm hungry."

CHAPTER
TWENTY-THREE

THEY WALKED TOGETHER to the cafeteria. But when they were about to go in, Arturo told him he'd catch him later. "I should be back at the library around seven-thirty if you want help going through those books."

"Thanks!" said Tom, though Arturo had already turned and was stalking away.

Tom saw his friends at their usual table. He dropped off his bag and made a beeline for the food counter. He was starving. Professor Montague had been kind in offering him lunch, but he normally ate a lot more for lunch and now he was feeling faint. He asked for double helpings of everything and the cafeteria attendant didn't even bat an eye. She heaped the food onto his plate and slid it over the counter.

Mandy sidled up to him and nudged him with her elbow. "Are you eating for two, Tom?"

He laughed and told her he had missed lunch.

"Yeah, we were wondering where you'd gotten off to. Did you get detention on your very first day? Or did you eat the sweets I warned you about and spend the lunch hour clutching your stomach over the toilet?"

"You weren't kidding about that?" asked Tom.

"No. Professor Filigree can be super mean when he wants to! Is that what happened?" she asked, putting a hand over her mouth. Tom couldn't tell if she was horrified or laughing. He saw the humor in her eyes and nudged her back.

"No! Professor Montague kept me after class for extra lessons."

"She's not allowed to do that. It's against the code. Students and faculty are allowed fifty minutes of uninterrupted time to rest and replenish at midday," she recited.

"You just made that up!" laughed Tom as he grabbed a piece of cheesecake and a bottle of water. Mandy took the same and they headed for the checkout to swipe their dining cards.

"No! It's in the school prospectus. Didn't you read it?"

Tom looked at her sideways, unsure if she was pulling his leg or not.

"I'm afraid I was not provided with a prospectus. I'll have to lodge a complaint with the student body president. Could you point me in the right direction?"

"You're in luck! I happen to be the student body vice-president," she said following him to their table.

When they sat down, Tom asked Benny to confirm what Mandy had said.

"Yeah, of course it's true," he replied.

Tom was quiet through dinner, mostly because he was busy packing away his food. The others chatted about their day, and they asked him about his first day.

"I learned a lot of stuff and I have a ton of homework. I'm probably going to hit the books after dinner."

"You've been inside all day, at least come out for a walk," said Zaina.

"What time is it?" he asked.

Benny checked his watch and replied, "It's only six-thirty. Besides, it'll be dark soon. We won't stay out too long."

Tom agreed and said he just wanted to drop off his bag as he'd been lugging it around all day.

Benny, Mandy, and Zaina were waiting on the steps outside the main entrance. When they saw Tom, they got up and the group moved toward a part of the grounds Tom hadn't visited yet. There was a well-worn path in the grass that followed a fenced-in field. In a few weeks, they'd be planting barley, but for now, the land looked desolate.

They walked for about ten minutes until they reached a stone circle. Not the kind where people gather for rituals or are transported into another time. No, this circle was man-made, and the stones had been carried and positioned around an unlit fire pit.

"When it's warmer, we light a fire and hang out here," explained Benny as they each took a seat on the rocks.

"Do you remember the duel I fought with Arturo?" asked Tom.

"Are you kidding?" said Benny, getting up again. "That was one of the highlights of the year!" he said gesticulating wildly.

"I'm surprised you don't have your own groupies, now," replied Zaina. "You certainly brought Arturo down a notch and, in doing so, earned most of the school's respect."

"Including Arturo's, I hope," said Tom, biting his lip.

"The fact that he even talks to you is proof that he knows you exist. Besides, he came to help in the battle, right?" said Mandy.

"If we asked him, do you think he could help us improve our dueling skills?" asked Tom.

Benny had sat back down, but now it was Zaina's turn to rise. "We don't need him. We can practice on our own!" She almost spat out the words. There was no love lost between Zaina and Arturo. Tom wondered if maybe they'd dated in the past, or if Arturo had brushed her off. If he had, he was an idiot.

"Get up. We can have our own little duel, right here. There's plenty of room, and we're even numbered," suggested Zaina.

Benny shot a look at Mandy. He looked unsure about the idea, and so did she. But she rallied and got up.

"Great idea! Which spells have you learned so far? Can you easily block?" asked Mandy.

Tom told her about the disarming spells he'd learned and said he had a pretty good handle on his shield now. "I think I can handle anything you throw at me."

Benny got up but remained mute, shuffling his feet. "Are you ok, Benny? You don't have to do it if you don't want to," said Tom.

"It's just that the last time you threw a rock, it ripped up a building a hundred feet away. I'm a little scared of what you can do to us if you lose control..."

He had a point.

"No Blood Magick. Just spells. I need to start doing regular magic. I don't have the kind of gifts you and Mandy have, but with a little practice, I should be able to use simple and complex spells. I mean, we had incantations at The Academy. They were small things, mostly to do with using a Door in unorthodox situations, but I could do them. Headmaster Lianon reminded me that Blood Magick isn't all I have to fight back with."

Mandy crossed her arms and cleared her throat. Tom continued, "even Mandy here suggested as much. I believe you said something like I should be working smarter not harder."

Mandy beamed and smiled smugly at the others.

"Okay, let's get on with it before we lose the light altogether. Mandy and Benny can face off first," said Zaina in her best battle sergeant voice. Benny and Mandy quickly did as she ordered and walked fifteen paces in opposite directions.

Once they were in position, Zaina said, "on your marks, get set, duel!"

Predictably, they both used their natural gift on each other. As a result, Benny was frosted over, and Mandy was immobilized. Tom laughed. "How do we unfreeze them?"

"Idiots! We said spells! Spells can easily be undone. Powers? That's an altogether other matter. Ugh!" replied Zaina and fished into her pocket. She pulled out a small cube. She spoke words in Latin that sounded familiar to Tom, though he couldn't place the meaning. She tapped the cube. It unfolded and expanded into a huge volume.

"Hey! I learned that at The Academy. I haven't used that incantation in a long time, but you've just reminded me how I can carry a book of spells around with me until I can memorize them!"

Zaina ignored him and tried to hold the book and page through it at the same time. "Come here," she snapped. Tom reluctantly obeyed. Zaina could be scary when she had that intense look in her eyes, but as he had done nothing to annoy her, he tried to relax.

"Hold your hands out," she said, and Tom complied. Perhaps it was part of a spell.

As it turned out, Zaina only wanted Tom to hold the book so she could use both hands to look through it.

"Glad to be of assistance," Tom said drily.

"It's a heavy book and you have nothing better to do," she replied.

The book didn't look like a textbook; most of the pages were hand-written. "Is that your family's grimoire?" Tom asked.

ZAINA NODDED AND GAVE A MUMBLE. She had found the page she was looking for and was tapping it. "This should do it."

She reached into her pocket again and pulled out a wand. "You have a wand?" asked Tom. When he saw the look he gave her, he regretted speaking. He'd never seen any of his friends use a wand. In class, only a handful of students had used wands. This was not the time to ask why.

Zaina went first to Benny. She pointed her wand at him and said "Quid unum magicae non sit alius solve."

The ice cracked and Benny shook off the excess. "Thanks, Zaina!" She gave him a stony stare and repeated the steps with Mandy. The girl lost balance and fell to the ground. "Thanks," she mumbled getting back to her feet.

"Are we having fun yet?" Zaina said and she stuffed the wand back into her pocket and stalked back to where Tom was still holding the book. She took the book and slammed it shut. She spoke the reverse incantation and the book folded itself back into a cube, which she pocketed.

"Show's over, we should get back inside," she said as she started for the path.

"But we haven't dueled yet!" replied Tom, throwing his hands in the air. Zaina kept walking.

Tom looked at Mandy and Benny. Benny was rubbing his hands along his arms and shivering. He shook his head and followed Zaina.

"It's getting dark. We can try again tomorrow if you want. Right after school so there's more daylight," suggested Mandy.

"Sure, I guess," shrugged Tom and followed the others, Mandy falling into step with him.

Tom asked Mandy what she had done over Spring break.

"I went home to Vermont. Spring is a bit of a yucky season there so my family and I went to a resort in Mexico. It was great!" she said.

As Mandy went on to describe the room she shared with her younger sister, Tom started to tune her out. Not from lack of interest, he was feeling anxious all of a sudden and he didn't know why. Like something bad was about to happen and he unconsciously started walking faster.

"Slow down Tom, I can't keep up with these tiny chicken legs," she said with a laugh, scrambling to keep up.

"Something's wrong," he said.

"What's wrong?"

"I don't' know," Tom replied looking back to the place they had left to see if anyone was following them.

Why am I so paranoid? I'm not wearing the ring, so that can't be the reason. There's no one back there.

He couldn't shake the feeling and scanned their surroundings. The field looked just like it had when they'd passed it before. Up ahead, he could see Benny, but he could no longer see Zaina. *Did she speed walk?*

He slowed his pace and Mandy finally caught up with him. She resumed her chattering and Tom started to relax. Whatever had gotten his hackles up was gone.

"So, you're saying that I can control other people because I can control their blood?" asked Tom incredulously, though Arturo had found a passage saying just that in one of the books he'd laid out for Tom to read.

"Yes," Arturo replied patiently, pulling out one of the books on magnetism and opening it to a chapter he'd tabbed with a sticky note. He tried to explain the science behind the phenomenon to Tom. At Tom's blank stare he said, "you know how you can lift and throw rocks through telekinesis, despite the fact that you don't actually have the telekinesis gift?"

"Uh, yeah," said Tom waiting to see where Arturo was going with this.

"We assumed it was because you were pushing minuscule blood particles that got attached to the objects when you came into contact with them. You are, in effect, controlling your blood and directing it outside your body. As a Blood Mage, you can control other people's blood as well. That's how you can heal them. You are telling their blood to produce more white blood cells, to heal whatever is wrong. And the process happens in the same way the body would normally heal itself if it had enough life force to do so. That's where you come in, you are sending energy, in addition to the healing message, and the force of it speeds up the healing process."

"That kind of makes sense. But what about the raising people from the dead thing? All the books and movies I read were very clear; Necromancy is a bad thing."

"That one is a little more complex. And you're right, I would never attempt it. Even if my own mother died. Once a soul leaves a body, whatever comes back isn't who inhabited the body before they died," said Arturo with a shiver.

Tom thought about the Blood Spear. He wasn't ready to share that with Arturo. But if anyone could find out more about such things, it would be him.

"Are there other things I could do?" asked Tom, flipping through one of the books about Blood Magick and rituals.

Arturo grabbed another book from the pile and flipped until he found another one of his sticky notes. "This one says you can use your blood in both offensive and defensive ways."

"That sounds a little vague…" replied Tom.

"Well, there was one case where a Blood Mage was attacked and, instead of producing an energy shield, his blood, and I quote, 'gathered into a disc, solidified, and stopped the arrow from entering the body'."

You mean to say that the Blood Mage's blood turned into an actual shield?" asked Tom, taking the book to read the passage for himself. Arturo reached over and pointed to the sticky note.

"Here, it says that the blood turned into a sword and the Mage was able to defeat over one hundred attackers," added Arturo.

"No way!" replied Tom, flipping to that part of the book to read it. There it was. Proof that he wasn't the only freak whose blood had congealed into a weapon.

Tom sat back and let go of the book. "Does it say anywhere how I became a Blood Mage? Is it genetic? Does it lay dormant until maturity?"

"It's usually passed down from father to son. But it can skip generations entirely since we haven't heard of a Blood Mage in hundreds of years," said Arturo. He grabbed another book from the pile.

"It says here," he flipped to one of the tabbed pages, "that the power can be stolen by draining a Blood Mage's blood."

Tom gulped. So that was The Master's intention, to drain Tom's blood and steal his power. "You mean he drinks it, like a vampire?"

Arturo looked at the passage and shrugged. "It doesn't say, but I'm assuming that they have to ingest it or get a transfusion of some kind to get the power," he said, placing a hand on Tom's shoulder. "Sorry, buddy."

Tom would spend the night dreaming about vampires draining his blood.

CHAPTER

TWENTY-FOUR

THE NEXT DAY WAS BUSY, though nothing out of the ordinary happened. Tom made sure to bring his Traveling Handbook to class so he could integrate those spells with the ones from his Spellcasting textbook.

That afternoon, he had an Economics class. It was unremarkable and the teacher, Professor Mendillo, gave a comprehensive if somewhat boring lecture.

After class, Tom had gone back to his room to do his homework. Though he was tempted to read the books waiting for him at the library, he still had homework to do, and it wouldn't do for him to start failing high school classes when he was supposed to be in university.

He also made sure to study both the Handbook and Spellcasting textbook.

When he joined his friends at dinner, he started to get into the routine of things. Benny joined him at the food counter, and they chatted about the upcoming Balancing Board tournament.

"You should really ask to join the team," he said.

"But it's well past mid-year. Surely, the team is set, and the Coach wouldn't want to have to train someone this late in the year."

"You never know, it's worth a shot. You're a natural."

"What's this?" asked Mandy, catching the tail end of their conversation. When Benny clued her in, Zaina looked up from her plate and shot daggers at him.

"Zaina doesn't want you to join the team as you might take her spot as the star player," he joked.

"Don't listen to this idiot. Of course, you should join the team if the Coach will have you. We need all the help we can get to beat the South American team. They're really good."

"Speaking of beating opponents, is there any chance of giving dueling another try after dinner?" Tom asked.

"Sure," said Zaina, "but if these two do something stupid again, I'm out!"

THEY WENT BACK to the stone circle and Tom got some good practice in. Against Mandy and Benny, he mostly used his shield to deflect whatever they sent at him. But with Zaina, he got a little bolder. She was a strong and capable Witch, and he didn't want her to think he was weak.

She still kicked his ass, even when he whipped out two of the new defensive spells, he'd learned in class that day. It was time for a break, and they sat down around the stone circle.

"Are your parents all-powerful Witches and Warlocks?" asked Tom to no one in particular.

"Both my parents came to school here," said Mandy. "There's a magic school closer to home, but Dad is from a long line of Scottish Warlocks, and he said it was tradition for us to go here."

"You mentioned you have a younger sister. Does she attend high school here? Would she be in any of my classes?" asked Tom.

"Yes, she's at the high school but she's only fifteen so I doubt you've bumped into her," replied Mandy.

"And what do your parents do for jobs?" he asked. She hadn't really answered his questions and he was curious. Were Witches and

Warlocks like Travelers? Did they basically live off their relatives' money?

"My Mom stayed home until Becky, that's my sister, started at Harding. Now, she teaches French at the University of Vermont. That's where she and my Dad met. He was teaching Gaelic to undergrads."

"That's fascinating. And your Dad, does he still teach at Uni?" Tom asked, genuinely interested.

"No, not anymore. My Dad works for the CEMB, now."

"Wait, really? What does he do?"

She blushed and put her head down. "You're going to think this is stupid."

"Whether it's stupid or not, now I HAVE to know," said Tom.

"He's a consultant regarding the Unseelie Court," she said, looking at Benny.

Tom looked at Benny. "What does that mean?"

"In Scottish Folklore, fairies are divided into two camps: the Seelie Court fairies are said to be human-friendly, warning them when they are in danger, asking for help when they cannot accomplish a task, and are generally thought to be happy and benign. The Unseelie Court fairies, are said to be the unholy fairies, those that seek to harm humans, the ones that steal babies and the like."

"You seem to know a lot about this, too," said Tom.

"My Mom's a Witch and my Dad's a Fairy," said Benny.

"Really?" Tom said, sitting up. "Will you be getting wings, then?" he asked, then felt bad and asked, "sorry, am I allowed to ask that?"

Benny chuckled and said, "you're allowed to ask about it, but you're not allowed to ask to see them."

"You mean to say you already have them?" asked Tom, completely flabbergasted. Wonder never ceased around this place.

Benny rose and stepped back so he'd have plenty of room. He put his hands out to his sides and started flapping them like wings then prancing around on tiptoes. Mandy and Zaina cracked up and started laughing and Tom knew he was being made a fool of.

"Ha, ha! I'm pretty sure what you just did is offensive to fairies," replied Tom.

Before he could reply, the earth shook, and Tom felt like someone had run up behind him. He turned quickly and saw no one.

Great, here we go again.

But he saw Mandy pull her feet off the ground like she'd just seen a mouse. Zaina's hand was on the ground, feeling for something.

"Is it an earthquake?" asked Benny just as the earth shook harder and the entire stone circle dropped six feet down into the earth. Benny only had time to jump back as the earth fell out from under his feet and his friends were no longer there.

Once he recovered from the shock, Benny peered over the edge and called out, "are you guys all right??"

There was a pause before Zaina replied, "just peachy."

"Tom? Mandy? Are you guys ok?" he asked.

"I'm ok!" yelled Mandy and Tom piped in, "me too!"

"I'm going to get help, hang in there!" he said and ran toward the school.

A FEW MINUTES LATER, Arturo was peering down at them with an amused smile. "Have you been using magic without supervision again, Tom?" he quipped.

"What are you doing up there? Is this your idea of a joke?" asked Zaina.

Arturo put a hand to his heart and gave his best impersonation of an affronted person.

"I know that you think I'm all-powerful, Zain, but I assure you, I cannot cause sinkholes."

"So, you just happened to pass by?" she said, her voice dripping with scorn.

"If you must know, I met Benny as he was dashing through the hall to the Headmistress' office. All he said was 'stone circle' and 'sinkhole.' I was sufficiently intrigued to come and investigate." It would be a while before Benny caught up to the group, having some rests along the way back after almost passing out from running so hard in the first place.

"You could get us out of here," said Zaina.

"I could. But then again, no one has asked nicely."

"Arturo, could you help us out of here?" said Tom.

"Yes, Tom. It would be my pleasure." Arturo hopped into the hole and levitated to the ground.

"Who's first?" he said, looking between Zaina and Tom.

"You should take Mandy, she doesn't like enclosed spaces," said Zaina.

"Of course. Mandy? Where are you?" asked Arturo.

"Quit joking around," said Zaina tersely.

"I'm not joking; she doesn't seem to be here," replied Arturo.

"She was here a minute ago," replied Tom, turning his head in all directions.

Zaina snapped her finger and manifested a flame at the end of her index finger. True enough, Mandy was nowhere to be found. They called her name, but she did not answer.

Zaina was pointing her finger and scanning the hole in a circular manner.

"Stop, go back," said Arturo. "There!"

There was a narrow tunnel leading away from the fallen stone circle, heading in the direction of the field. As it was close to the surface, Arturo levitated above ground to see if it led out to the surface. "There. A path of dirt through the field. Should we follow it?" he asked looking down at the others.

"Of course we should follow it!" exclaimed Zaina, immediately heading for the tunnel.

"Wait!"

"We don't have time to lose, Arturo. If someone's taken Mandy," said Tom, following on Zaina's heels.

"I see someone! They've just surfaced at the other end of the field," Arturo said, still hovering above the sinkhole. He rose higher to get a better view. "They're getting into a black car. They're speeding away!"

Arturo hovered down to Zaina and Tom's level. "Come on, get us out of here so we can follow them," she snapped at him.

"I'm not superman! I can't carry you both and chase after a car!" he said.

He hit Tom on the arm. "Ouch. What was that for?"

"Do the Door thing," said Arturo.

"Yes! Tom, open a Door to wherever Mandy is going!" said Zaina, excited now.

"I'm not a mind reader. I can only go to where someone is, not where they're planning on going," he said.

"Who cares, just follow Mandy!"

Tom looked unsure but he took out his Key and his Door appeared. He closed his eyes, took a deep breath, and thought of Mandy.

"Here goes nothing," he said and opened the Door, Zaina, and Arturo following close behind.

CHAPTER
TWENTY-FIVE

THEY WERE in Mandy's dorm room. Thankfully, her roommate wasn't in the room, otherwise there would have been hell to pay.

"Focus on where Mandy is NOW," said Zaina. Her tone was unhelpful, and it was stressing Tom out.

"She got into a long black car, not quite a limousine, but a town car or some such," said Arturo. "Picture her in a black car, speeding away to The Master's lair."

Tom didn't care for the image, but he tried to picture Mandy riding in the back of a car. He called his Door and they tried again.

This time, they came out just behind a gas station, near the outer toilets.

"Maybe she needed to pee, and they stopped," said Zaina, running around the side of the building to the front of the store.

She came back before the others could follow suit. "If they did, they've gone now."

Tom called his Door again and pictured Mandy, imagining her school uniform.

They were in a dense forest. Tom closed the Door and it disappeared. The night was clear, and the moonlight gave them just enough light to see.

"Where are we?" asked Tom.

Arturo pointed ahead through the trees. "I think we've found The Master's lair."

It was a large mansion, or perhaps a small castle, depending on how you looked at it. Moving closer, they saw it was surrounded by a tall stone wall, at least eight feet, maybe ten.

"Can you see above the wall?" asked Tom, keeping his voice down. What he meant was, can you levitate and check it out, but he thought that might be too pushy.

"Yeah, sure. I'll find a tall tree I can hide behind, so no one sees me," replied Arturo. He scanned the area and found a tree that would fit the bill. He rose slowly until he was higher than the wall by a few feet and found a branch to rest on while he looked around.

He got off the branch, lowered his position, and moved sideways toward another tree, then went back up to check things out.

He repeated the process once more, further down the wall before he came back.

"There are Warlocks posted at every door, and at least two on the roof," he said pointing in the direction he had seen the guards. "I think they're expecting you."

"But they're not expecting *us!*" replied Zaina, jabbing at herself, her eyes those of a fearless warrior.

"Woah there," whispered Arturo. "This is no time to be going off half-cocked."

"Of course, you would say that," spat Zaina.

"What's that supposed to mean?" snapped Arturo.

"You know exactly what that means," replied Zaina, getting in his face.

"Um, guys?" interrupted Tom, putting a hand on each of their shoulders.

Yeah, there's something going on there, he thought.

"I don't know what *this* is?" Tom whispered waving his hands around to include them both, "but we need a plan."

"That's easy. We go in there, grab Mandy, and get out."

"What about the guards?" asked Tom.

"We can take them, no problem. We've done it before," she said.

She sounded so confident that, for a minute, Tom would have followed her into any battle.

Fortunately, Arturo interrupted his wild imaginings. "Sorry to be the voice of reason here, but it's one thing to take on an opponent on your own turf where help can arrive any minute. It's another thing to go into what is obviously a trap, in a location we don't know anything about, where an unknown number of possible assailants lie in wait."

He was right, of course. What could the three of them accomplish against The Master's army of minions in a castle that might be booby-trapped.

"But what about Mandy?" asked Tom, anxious to get his friend out of harm's way.

"We don't even know if she's in there," replied Arturo.

"The Door led us here," said Zaina.

"Right, but it led us to two other places before we got here. What if they came here only to go elsewhere?" asked Arturo.

It was a reasonable question. They'd have to determine if Mandy was in the castle or not before anything else.

"Well then go hover around the windows until you find her," said Zaina, waving her hand in the air toward the castle.

"It might be dark, but I'm not exactly invisible, am I? Also, there could be wards above the walls. And even if there weren't, they could be keeping Mandy underground," he said tersely. He seemed to be running out of patience with Zaina.

"You mean like in a dungeon?" asked Tom. This was like Tabitha all over again.

"Tom, can't you open a Door to where Mandy is?" asked Zaina. Her bravado was slipping. Tom thought she might be imagining Mandy in a cold, wet, scary dungeon too.

"No, I can't open a Door into private homes or buildings. If we ended up here in the woods, I'd say the odds are high there are wards around the wall."

"Then how can we find out if she's in there or not?" she asked.

"When Tabitha was kidnapped, we found her using a locator spell. Once we knew her position, Professor Montague used astral projection to go check on Tabitha and pinpoint her location. Can either of you astral project?" he asked.

"Technically, anyone can astral project with enough practice and focus. But only gifted Witches and Warlocks can do it at will and control where they go and how long they stay," replied Arturo.

"I'm guessing neither of you are so gifted, then?" he asked. They shook their heads.

He knew Lola and Devlin could do it, but they were at The Academy. Tom couldn't go there and, even if he sent them a Traveling letter, he doubted they would sneak out to come help him. More than likely, they'd get the Headmaster and he'd call Miss Clementine, and they would probably suggest the same course of action as they had when Tabitha was taken.

"Do you have a locator spell in your grimoire? So we can determine if she's still here?" asked Tom.

"I know how to do the spell without the book. What I don't have is a map and something of hers to scry with," said Zaina.

"We can try the Door again," suggested Tom.

"Yeah, let's do that. Worse case we end up back here again," said Arturo.

Tom pulled out his Key, thought of Mandy, and just before he would normally have opened the Door, he said the spell that made a window appear so they could look out. It was a useful spell for unknown, public, or potentially crowded locations. The Door remained invisible to anyone in the target destination and Travelers could determine if it was safe to open the Door. They peered through the window and saw the castle, but from a different angle.

"Should we try it?" asked Tom.

"Yeah. It might give us more intel," said Zaina.

Tom turned the handle, and they went through.

They were still in the woods around the castle but were faced with a side view.

"Do you think that means Mandy's in there, on this side of the castle?" asked Tom.

"I think we should do it a few times more until we keep coming to the same spot," said Arturo.

Begrudgingly, Zaina said that was smart. But she also suggested that Arturo do a little recon on this side of the castle. The more they knew about the castle, the better it would be. They assumed they were still in Scotland, but they could be anywhere. Without any geographical markers, or a phone handy, there was no telling where they were.

"I wish I had my phone," said Tom. "Why do they ban cell phones at magic school? Don't they know how useful they are?"

"I know, right! I could be taking areal pics," replied Arturo as he rose from the ground.

While he was doing his thing, Zain answered Tom's question. "In addition to phones being banned in most schools for the usual reasons, they are banned at magic school because they interfere with our ability to use magic and with the ley lines. The electromagnetic charge scrambles the frequency. I'm sure nerd boy over there could explain it better."

Tom nodded, remembering the books on electromagnetism waiting for him at the library. Just when he'd finally found useful books, this had to happen. Would he never have the time to prepare, to train? Would he just have to wing it and hope for the best?

"What's the deal between you two?" Tom asked. "You don't seem to like each other very much. Did something happen?"

Zaina shrugged and turned to look up at Arturo. He was coming back toward them; the story would have to wait.

"There are guards posted near the doors on this side too. I couldn't see the ones on the roof from here."

Tom opened another Door and they saw the same view from this window.

"I guess she's in there, then," said Zaina. "Now what?"

"I hate to say it, but we need to go back to school and ask for help," said Tom.

THE END

If you enjoyed this book, please consider leaving a review on Amazon, Bookbub, or Goodreads?

Reviews help me reach new readers and improve my craft.

Read *Blood Legacy*, the final book in the ***Blood Magick Trilogy!***

www.ingramcontent.com/pod-product-compliance
Lightning Source LLC
Chambersburg PA
CBHW020337260626
47156CB00004B/1570